Biggles over Baghdad

by

James Conor O'Brien

ISBN-10: **1519529023**
ISBN-13: **9781519529022**

To Lachlan Brown

who while lost in the jungle of his kitchen
saved a kitten called Biggles from a paper bag
bravest fool I ever knew.

Biggles gives a Pre-Flight Briefing

"Men," said the wing commander.

"And women," came a gruff woman's voice.

"I thought you were one of the Kuwaitis?" asked the wing commander.

"I am."

"Hmmm, anyway," continued the wing commander unperturbed, "Men, women and other members of the squadron of unknown sex. You must remember we are at war."

"It's hard to forget," said Ginger, "they keep shooting at us."

"Now none of that." The wing commander wagged his stick at Ginger. "Foreigners have been shooting at the R.A.F. ever since its inception. So, the present circumstances are no different, except of course, we have the Americans on our side."

"Half the time," Ginger insisted, "it is the Americans who are doing the shooting."

"Yes, that is what we call friendly fire." The wing commander smiled paternally, "So shooting at us - is how the jolly Americans show they are being friendly. It's like fox hunting, we don't really want to kill the fox and half the time the little blighters get away. So, next time an F-16 starts blazing away at you, just hide behind a hedge and wait for the hunt to lose your trail."

"They killed Nigel."

"Nigel was a vegetarian. Shouldn't have been flying in the first place." The wing commander blew through his moustache in annoyance. "Now this war…"

"I thought this was a police action," asked Algy, "like those times in Korea when we rescued Korea from itself, and in Vietnam when we didn't rescue anyone, we just got shot at."

"Those too were police actions, but this time, we have a plan."

"We do?" asked Algy in complete amazement.

"Yes," the wing commander almost chortled, "the plan is we are appearing to lose, but in reality we are not. Therein lies the beauty of the plan. Its very nature is a cipher, an enigma, and a code if you will. Hence our enemies can not determine our next course of action."

"But we are losing," whined Algy, "Iraq has fallen apart, the different factions and clans commit atrocities every night; and we can't even leave the base without someone taking pot-shots at us. How is that winning?"

"Misère."

"Sorry, what?"

"Misère," the wing commander banged his stick on the blackboard where it was written, "it's where in Five Hundred or Canasta you choose to lose every hand and in so doing win the game."

A mosquito could have burped in the debriefing room and it would have been heard.

"But, but," Algy began tearing his cap in two in frustration, "how is that winning? Iraq isn't a card game!"

"Yes!" the wing commander was triumphant, "and not only does our enemy not know it's a card game, they also don't even know how to play Five Hundred or Canasta! We cannot lose! Unless, of course if we win."

"But Wing Commander," Algy almost started to cry, "don't we have to declare at the beginning of the hand, that we are going to play Misère?"

"What?" the wing commander shrieked back. "And give away the element of surprise? Haven't you read Carl von Clausewitz and his idea of the Fog of War? The enemy isn't supposed to know what we are doing, that's half the plan!"

"But this isn't a war! It's a ...well it's bally well not a war."

"Which is also what we want the enemy to think."

"But, but, but," Algy was reduced to saying over and over.

"So, now that that is all settled. Captain Biggles will now address you on today's bombing run and answer any of your questions," the wing commander finished sat down and promptly fell asleep.

Biggles stood up, pulled the goggles back from his eyes and stared at his fellow pilots with the sort of intensity you'd expect from a short man with a moustache at Nuremberg.

"Men," he declared looking out the window with a fierceness that would have frightened that short man with a moustache at Nuremberg, "we have not come here to crush our enemies. We have not come here to lead them to the promised land. We have not come here to hand out ice cream and lollipops. No, we are here because we are British, and the British have never needed a reason to invade another country, except when we invaded Germany, or France and occasionally America, but lets ignore those for the moment. We have come here to win a war so let us concentrate on the problem at hand."

He turned around and looked at the map of Iraq, then searched around till he found Norway and pointed at that.

"This is our target."

"Norway?"

"Oh sorry," he tried again and found Iran. "This is our target."

"But we're not at war with Iran."

"We soon will be," Biggles looked down his nose at his interlocutor, "and when it happens, we will not only be ready, but we will have already attacked them. I too, have read Carl von Clausewitz."

"Isn't he a Hun?"

"Is he?" Biggles said in some surprise, "I thought he was Welsh, odd name and all."

"Quite sure, born June 1, 1780, died November 16, 1831, a Prussian soldier, military historian and influential military theorist. Noted for his work titled 'On War'."

"Algy, don't be such a girly swat." Biggles snapped. "I'm giving the briefing. Besides he may be a Hun and all, but that doesn't mean I can't read him. Now then, our reconnaissance shows us that Iran is filled with Persian carpets; in fact, Iran oddly enough is where all Persian carpets come from. It is one of the primary industries of Iran. Carpets are made from wool, and wool comes from sheep. These will be our targets. We are going to destroy all the sheep in Iran and cripple their economy. I read this in Clausewitz and he would know."

The only sound that could be heard for several minutes was the wind blowing against the tent flap.

"No questions, good," said Biggles pleased, "random bombing will start at 0500 hours, and continue till we run out of air-to-sheep missiles. Dismissed."

Saddam of Arabia

Saddam tested the water with his toe, it was just right, not too cool that he needed to hang his masseur and not too warm that he needed to drown his hair stylist. With lugubrious sigh he sank into a blue pool sprinkled with rose petals and longed for the old days when ruling the great Iraqi nation was a doddle. Outside cruise missiles crashed into the palace garden's of Saddam City, tracer fire raced across the sky, A-10 Thunderbolt II Warthogs screamed past firing long blurps with their GAU-8 Avenger Gatling guns 30 millimetres rounds simply demolishing tanks and buildings in seconds. Saddam push his earplugs in deeper and hoped the noise would go away.

He picked up his favourite book, Goethe's 'The Sorrows of Young Werther' randomly opened the part where young Werther kills himself, and quickly dropped it back on the marble. Then he remembered the lion of the desert would never die in a such an undignified way, no Saddam Hussein Abd al-Majid al-Tikriti the Magnificent would go out in a blaze of glory on the battlefield riding a white horse and charging his enemy with a sword, the idea he might die some mediocre death was impossible. He pulled out his gold plated sword and swished about the pool with it. Then opened the book again and read from another random page.

"I wait for the morning of my tears."

He tried to cry but discovered he had forgotten how, so he simply made a small moue with his mouth and pushed his rubber giraffe about the pool.

Outside his world was collapsing about him, but he had seen off worse threats to his regime, like the time the all girls skating team had defected to Finland, or the time his cabinet had forgotten to order pizza so he had them bulldozed into the Euphrates. At least here, inside his Al-Faw Palace he was happy, the tranquil waters of the great lagoon reflecting the afternoon sun and swallows dipping their beaks and nesting in the alcoves. Here, behind high walls and a huge moat he could put aside all the petty troubles of being a great warrior.

Saddam held a hand to his brow, sighed and looked tragic. He found another quote Goethe and read it aloud dramatically, "Nothing is more dangerous than solitude." He sighed, looked out the window. Then stood up stark naked, picked up a rifle and shot one of his gardeners before yelling, "I said tulips, you idiot! Not pansies!"

In the air above Baghdad, Biggles had accidentally run into one of the American cruise missiles about to land on Saddam palace, so technically it didn't count as getting shot down, more of a friendly crash than a definite kill to the Americans. He also noted it was the middle of the night, so a chap really wouldn't be expected to blind sided by a Tomahawk cruise missile even if it was the middle of a battlefield.

He found himself parachuting over a city on fire, tracers seemed to fall upwards filling the sky with strange tendrils of lights that were interposed with huge flashes and columns of smoke."I know this music," Biggles grinned. Then remembered he was parachuting right into it. The bangs was so loud his whole body rattled with concussion and he had to blink to see after each flash. "And it's a bit too Wagnerian for my liking."

With a rush he found himself falling into the centre of a lake which conveniently for him had a housing estate on a island, after a moments recce in the light of the bomb flashes he realized it was a bit too Island of Wight to be considered a housing estate and more of a grand palatial hotel with ack-ack guns. He landed on the top of Saddam's palace surrounded by Republican Guards and wondered if he should have phoned ahead for a reservation. The guards, however, were too busy to notice him, firing ack-ack at mostly empty sky in the vain hope of downing a Tomahawk missile, which was pointless as the missiles were really coasting along just above the streets and stopping at traffic lights on the way to their targets.

"Spiffing," Biggles stepped free of his parachute, before wandering over and punching out the guards on the ack-ack guns. He looked around to see if anyone was watching, remembered he hated competition, then jumped on the gun and shot down the next Tomahawk missile he saw while shaking his fist, "And let that be a lesson!"

All was chaos in the third night of the Baghdad bombing, most of the chaos was due to Biggles who had been tasked with flying low level sorties to route the Republican guard from their foxholes before he had accidentally come a cropper with the American missile. Now that he was out of the sky things were starting to settle down barring the odd massive explosion, endless friendly fire on the side of the Iraqis and the Iraqi national anthem blaring out on the speakers throughout Baghdad. Most of the city was out of their houses watching the fireworks, since according to their Minister of Information the Americans were nowhere near Baghdad and had been driven into the sea, apparently what the populace was seeing was celebration of a great victory over the imperialists.

"I wonder if they have crumpet?" Biggles muttered to himself and found a door leading downstairs.

In the depths of morning Saddam met with his war council and discussed reports from the war front.

"Oh illustrious one! Light of the moon!" his Information Minister Muhammed Saeed al-Sahaf waved his hands wildly, "we have driven the cursed dogs of America into the sea and captured Detroit!"

Information Minister Muhammed Saeed al-Sahaf, who was better known to the West as 'Baghdad Ali' was not known for his geographical accuracy but very well known for his theatrical predictions of America's impending destruction, and had got the job by always saying what his president wanted to hear.

"Our Detroit or their Detroit?" Saddam was genuinely puzzled and looked out the window at a destroyed city, "at the present moment we have a lot more Detriots than they do!"

"We have captured all Detriots," Saeed al-Sahaf beamed, "ours and theirs!"

"Excellent," Saddam grinned, "with their Detroit in our possession, America will bow down to our demands. By the way, what are our demands?"

"America must submit to the will of Saddam Hussein Abd al-Majid al-Tikriti, Field Marshal of the Universe, Divine Light of the President of Republic of Iraq and the Chairman of Revolutionary Command Council, Supreme..."

"Just get to the point," Saddam tapped the desk in annoyance.

"All American troops will surrender to ours, the American states of Kansas, Greenland and Mexico shall be given in perpetuity to the the Iraqi people and the sum of not less than thirty trillion Iraqi dinar shall be paid over a period of two years to the Royal Bank of Baghdad, with two hundred percent interest on default."

"How much is that in American dollars?"

"About four hundred and thirty five dollars and eight cents."

"That much? Excellent." Saddam's eyes gleamed with a sense of righteousness, as outside a cruise missile destroyed his duck pond. "We will make them pay or my name is not Saddam Hussein. Why Kansas?"

"Kansas is in the heart of America." Saeed al-Sahaf rose up to his full five four and twitched his moustache. "Once we have our armies in Kansas we will be able to strike at them in every direction at any time in the future, then they will never dare attack us again."

Saddam nodded and smiled at his chief minister. "You have done well, and what is their reply?"

"They dared to laugh at me, and wanted to know if instead of Kansas we will take Brazil? "

"Hmm. Is Brazil part of America?"

"Yes light of the dawn, I looked it up on Google-Earth."

"Is Brazil bigger than Kansas?"

"Yes supreme leader," Saeed al-Sahaf stretched his arms out wide, "much, much bigger."

"Good then," Saddam was satisfied, "tell the Americans we will accept their surrender when they stop bombing my palaces. For their insolence to you we will take both Kansas and Brazil or destruction will fall upon them for a thousand years."

"So shall it be written in the stars."

Biggles was wandering around the Presidential Palace with a candle trying to find phone. No one paid any attention to him, as in the dark they just imagined he was one of their pilots. The Al-Faw Palace was ornate beyond belief, black marble columns rose to ceilings in vivid red and green from which hung enormous chandeliers forty foot in diameter, the floor was so polished Biggles could see his reflection in the candle light. Massive marble spiral staircases covered with monograms of Saddam's initials rose up into the darkness, lead to an interior pool sparkling with faux gems.

"It just like Empire Day in Birmingham," Biggles thought to himself.

Guards scurried past him carrying booty before the Americans or even the Iraqi people stole them, strange things like bidets, basket ball hoops and paintings of Saddam frolicking in the moonlight with ribbons and fauns. Biggles turned a corner and came face to face with Saddam, who was cradling a gold plated Kalashnikov watching a film in his library.

It was his favourite movie, Saddam of Arabia, it was identical in all scenes and dialogue to the original Lawrence of Arabia film, only it had a Saddam Hussein double in place of Lawrence and was dubbed into Arabic. It was the scene where Lawrence/Saddam arrives in Cairo and tells Brighton he has taken Aqaba.

-We've taken Aqaba!- Saddam mouthed the words and ate popcorn.

Brighton: -Taken Aqaba? Who has?-

Saddam: -We have. Our side in this war has. The wogs have. We have...-

"Who left wogs in the script?" Saddam fired the Kalashnikov at the ceiling. "I swear to god I will evaporate them."

Brighton: -You mean the Americans have gone?-

Saddam: -No, they're still there but they've no boots. Prisoners, sir. We took them prisoners, the entire American army. No, that's not true. We killed some, too many really. I'll manage it better next time. There's been a lot of killing, one way or another. Cross my heart and hope they die, it's all perfectly true.-

Brighton: -It isn't possible.-

Saddam: -Yes it is. Saddam did it.-

Biggles stumbled into the projectionist and the film clattered to a halt. The silence was devastating until Saddam murdered the screen with his gun.

"Who stopped me in mid-scene? I just took Aqaba!"

Everyone pointed at Biggles who pointed at everyone else.

"You there! Who are you?"

"I did," Biggles' pluck and dash came to the fore, "I'm Biggles. I'm British."

"Well I'm Saddam, I am Iraq, all of Iraq would follow me to death."

"What have you done for Iraq? Why should your people follow you?"

"Because I am a river to my people!" Saddam replied. "You are an Englishman. Are you not loyal to England?"

"An Englishman is always loyal to England, it's England being loyal to all Englishmen that's the hard bit." Biggles snarled. "Give up Saddam you can not win. History will besmirch your name!"

"All extraordinary men, who have accomplished great and astonishing actions, have ever been decried by the world as drunken or insane," Saddam retorted.

"Which are you?"

"Thine mother mated with a scorpion," Saddam stuck his Kalashnikov in Biggles face, "for this you die!"

At that moment, one of those annoying American Tomahawk cruise missile removed the ceiling and most of the plaster. In the ensuing melee Biggles ran off with Saddam's gold plated sword and made a small fortune on Antiques Roadshow with it.

Biggles the Legend

"Well, Mister Saddam," Biggles grinned wildly, "it's time to see how fast you can ride a camel!"

Biggles had turned up late for a briefing on the War in Iraq and was now convinced that everyone in Iraq was called Saddam, this made mission coordination difficult at the best of times. He tore down on the battlefield like Beckham coming in for the final goal at Webley. The ground erupted in long lines of destruction, as thousands of rounds of tracer fire blew holes through houses, cars and screaming gunmen. Very quickly as what had been an assault on the enemy forward observation post dissipated into carnage and anybody remotely called Saddam vanished, the battle abruptly came to a complete halt.

"Biggles," the voice of a fellow pilot echoed in his ears, "You really must come and play tennis sometime, I need a good partner."

"Only too happy to, old man," Biggles grinned in his oxygen mask, "but first…"

"You blithering idiot!" the voice of Group Captain Wilkinson thundered across the airwaves as a Typhoon jet shot meters above Biggles' Harrier-jet at Mach one. "That was my kill!"

"Sorry old boy," Biggles grinned even wider, as he guided his craft back behind across the Tigris into a safe zone, "saw an opportunity and pounced."

With that he switched frequencies back to wide spectrum and started listening for more 'opportunities' as he called them. Biggles flew his Harrier-jet in the same way helicopter pilots flew their choppers. Bouncing and jumping about the battle zone, dropping in and out, and given the need roaring up the Machs of the Rolls-Royce Pegasus 107 engine to charge in like a shark at Bondi Beach just after the tourists had dipped their toes. He was the devil in the sky.

A report came over of a line of tanks moving through the desert headed for the Kuwait border. Biggles did an Immelmann manoeuvred flipped back into the opposite direction before roaring into Mach one with the afterburner. A few minutes later, he saw in the distance the unmistakable plumes of smokes from Russian tanks making their way south. This was all encouragement Biggles needed, he flew up to get into an attack dive, then fell upon the convoy like an eagle in a dove cot. It was only after he had flown away he noticed all the tanks were empty, little more burning shells left over from an American attack the previous day and the troops long gone.

"Blast!" Biggles swore, then marked down on his kill sheet a dozen Russian T-72s, glad he didn't have a wingman on his shoulder to correct him. Biggles didn't need a wingman, they only got in the way of how amazing he was, the sky wasn't big enough when Biggles was on the hunt. He was such an extraordinary pilot that RAF Air Command had once considered making him the only pilot in a squadron, but it was decided that a lone Biggles in the sky was simply too dangerous weapon to leave lying around and the other pilots were there to rein him in. After all, this was the pilot who during the Blitz landed in Paris, punched out Goering and then kidnapped the Folies Bergère. He was dangerous, yes, but not someone you let out of your sight, which is why as often as he could he sneaked off from the airbase for a bit of fun as he called it.

For reasons that nobody understood, Biggles was now immortal, after being shot over nine thousand times, and dying up to thirty-five times, he had somehow gained immortality. It was such a mystery that the medicos were known to have nervous breakdowns whenever he walked in for a check up.

"But you have to be one hundred and three years old," Captain Mortimer gasped, "It's just not possible."

"Hundred and six," Biggles grinned, somehow managing a deaths head grin, "but whose counting?"

"I am!" Mortimer shrieked. "You shouldn't even be flying!"

"Where there is danger, whenever Britain sends out a need for volunteers," Biggles stood to attention, "I'll be there."

"But you're dead."

"Old Blighty needs me."

"No, we don't," argued Mortimer hopelessly, "We're fighting peasant boys, armed with twenty-year-old Kalashnikov and pick up trucks. The kill ratio is over a thousand to one. We can't possibly lose."

"Traitor!" Biggles spat, then pulled out his .455 Webley Mark I service revolver and shot Mortimer in the thigh. "Physician, heal thyself."

Over the years Biggles had shot over fifteen medicos in the leg. It was his way of dealing with the madness of war.

"You shot me?" Mortimer gasped in disbelief.

"Flesh wound." Biggles retorted. "Take two aspirins and don't see me in the morning. Hate waking up to strange men in my tent."

"You shot me?" Mortimer still couldn't get this singular fact into his world view.

"Look, old man," Biggles scratched his own ear with the barrel of his Webley, "I'm Biggles, you know Bigglesworth, famous flying Ace, hero of the Ardennes, warrior of the Wehrmacht, sturmtrooper of Stalingrad and all that."

At that moment the regimental band happened to wander by, as it always did when Biggles got literary, and began playing Land of Hope and Gory.

"This isn't about me, it's about Queen, the Empire and cricket at Lords, for there will always be an England. No matter what the danger, a true Englishman will step up to the thin red line, shoulder to shoulder we will stare the fuzzy-wuzzys in the eye and send them to the netherworld. Should the Empire be threatened, should the Australians win the Ashes, should the tea be cold, the Biggles will be there."

"You shot me?" Mortimer sank to the floor.

"Look, are you going to pass me as fit, or do I have to get all Panacea on your Hippocratic Oath?"

The myth of Biggles had grown so great that even he believed in it.

His Harrier-jet coasted along the river deftly weaving through the sand dunes, for all the world a bird of prey searching for mice and snakes as Biggles liked to think of them. Tracer fire occasionally erupted about him, but this was just what Biggles wanted, as it gave the exact location of his quarry and he would roar his twin Rolls-Royce Pegasus 107 engines and flip onto his back. Blasting away with the GAU-12/U Equalizer, a five-barrel 25 mm Gatling gun-style rotary cannon, to give them a bit of his mind.

Sometimes he almost landed on top of the enemy, just to roast them with the down blast of the jets. Biggles didn't hate anyone, he was too well brought up for such a petty emotion, it was he just didn't recognize the enemy as people; more along the lines of fast moving targets with legs. Once he had closed in, there was no hope for Mister Saddam as he called all of them, who simply couldn't run or dig fast enough, and shooting back at Biggles only made him annoyed, as it meant more holes in the airframe to patch up.

Once he flown so low, he had sanded away the paint and ripped off half the avionics of his plane. Which in turn, annoyed him so much he parked the jet, got out and gave Mister Saddam a good thrashing; then dragged the poor fellow by the ear and pointed out all the damage that had been done to the plane, the poor fellow was so shocked he offered to clean the windscreen. With Biggles in the air the British Empire could never lose.

Debriefing Biggles

Biggles reported to the debriefing tent after his skirmishing and met Group Captain Wilkinson. Group Captain Wilkinson wore a lugubrious expression worthy of Wellington being told his entire army had diarrhoea just before the battle of Waterloo.

"Biggles," sighed Wilkinson, "I have a report you bombed Iran again, is this true?"

"Possibly," Biggles grinned ecstatically, "where is it?"

"In the same place as you bombed last time, you know the borders of countries don't tend to move too often."

"Yes, sir," Biggles looked thoughtful, "is it filled with those funny looking chaps with the towels on their heads and camel jockeys hidden in their dresses?"

"No, those are our allies," the Group Captain sighed, "The Saudis and the Kuwaitis, remember half our squadron is made up of them. No, Iranians wear immaculate black suits, don't shave and never wear ties. And in general, they live somewhere north of where we are standing. You know, the ones that captured you, put you up in a hotel for nine days, and played backgammon with you, after you bombed and landed on the wrong airfield …yet again."

"Oh those Blighters!" Biggles looked annoyed. "Well, jolly well I should say so, I give them a taste of their own medicine."

"But they haven't bombed us, they haven't done anything to warrant our bombing them. And it says here, you attacked a field of sunflowers and a donkey. Is that true?"

Biggles looked puzzled.

"I thought it was a radar installation. Could have been, those tricky blighters are rather well - tricky aren't they?"

The Group Captain looked at Biggles with the same expression of weariness of roman general might have had when he realized his insane, drunken barbarian auxiliaries were all he had to hold back all the insane, drunken barbarians who were about to invade Rome itself.

"Biggles."

"Yes Sir!" Biggles yelled enthusiastically.

"I have another report that says you shot a flock of geese."

"Ah, yes sir, sun was in my eyes and what. Won't happen again."

"They were in a barn in Turkey."

"G.P.S. was playing up sir. I got confused with the difference between geese and turkeys."

"So you…" the pause would have been worthy of Kenneth Branagh delivering the soliloquy of Hamlet, "…destroyed a barn in an neutral country with an Amraam missile. Biggles you're not even supposed to have Amraams on your plane."

"I put it on for ballast, sir!"

"Why," the Group Captain sighed once more, "or perhaps I shouldn't ask, no, I feel like an adventure, why, oh why did you need ballast on a jet plane?"

"I've been experimenting with submarines, I'm trying to see if I can take off from under the sea. Jolly clever what? Saw it on the Thunderbirds. I say, sir when can I have one of those rockets things?"

"They're not real Biggles, and I suspect you're not real either."

"Thank you sir!" Biggles saluted.

The tent was filled with aircrew, subalterns, communications officers, and ground crew who always came to watch one of Biggles amazing debriefings. He never ceased to astound one and all with his endless ability to take a perfectly rational argument and turn it into a hopelessly insane monologue about how amazing he was. For days afterwards the aircrews would gather around open fires and bars and regale each with the latest stories, all of them secretly hoping to emulate this titan of chaos, this man of mayhem.

"I have another report you shot down a German medical transport, is this true?"

"Yes sir! They went down faster than a choirboy at Malton College."

"The German's are our allies, you know, the whole NATO thingy. We're not supposed to shoot them, it annoys them."

"They are?" Biggles looked as puzzled a ferret that just been run over by a truck and ended up in the carburettor. "What happened to that Hitler chappy?"

"Biggles, tell me why I shouldn't have you shot for insubordination?"

"I'm British."

"Yes?"

"It wouldn't be British to shoot me, I'm British. Sir!"

"Biggles, you know I'd send you to Afghanistan just to get rid of you, but I know full well you'd end up starting World War Three with the Russians," the Group Captain wrote something down, "so I want you to have another psychological check up."

"Another? But sir, that's the fourteenth this month and it's only the second of May," Biggles protested.

"Yes, and the more check ups you have, the less time you spend in the air."

"But sir!" Biggles pleaded.

"Biggles," Wilkinson smirked slyly, "it's for Blighty."

"Yes sir!" Biggles saluted, "for old Blighty."

Whereupon he spun on the spot and marched out of the tent to the loud applause of his fellow pilots and ground crew, he was worth more in entertainment value then the world rugby competition being hosted at the Folies Bergère.

Biggles' Psychological Assessment.

"Sit down Captain," the psychologist motioned to Biggles to use the couch.

"Thanks Algy, but will there be crumpet?"

"No, now lie down."

"Finger biscuits?"

"No, now lie down, that's an order."

"We're both captains, you can't order me."

"I'm also a doctor, so I can."

"I'm a pilot, so you can't."

"Okay," the psychologist sighed, " very well – no, hang on, I'm a pilot too, that means I still outrank you."

"I'm a pilot and an ace."

"We're both aces."

"True but come to think of it, I'm also Biggles, nobody outranks a Biggles."

"The group captain does."

"He does?" frowned Biggles, "and all this time I thought he just signed the pay-checks. Got to respect the paymaster you know."

"Very well, stand there if you must, but for heavens sake answer these bally questions."

"Algy, you can't make me stand for hours on end, that's a form of torture." Biggles grinned and lay down on the couch. "More childhood?"

"If you like." Algy made a scribble. Algy or 'Algernon Lacey' was in fact a cousin of Biggles, but they always started the counselling in a semi-professional way, just to show good form.

"Algy, we grew up together, don't you already know everything about my childhood?" Biggles rested his arms behind his head.

"That's not the point old man, you have to talk about it, that way you might think of something or other."

"Something or other what?"

"I don't know, we won't know until you bally well talk about it."

"So how will we know when I am talking about it?" Biggles eyebrows collapsed like the wings of a Fokker Dr.I triplane after Manfred von Richthofen had missed the runway.

Algy pulled a book from behind him, and leafed through the pages. Algy wasn't really a psychologist, but it gave him something to do while he was convalescing. He too had been shot so many times that it was a miracle he was still alive, and now spent most of his time lying around trying to get the use of legs back - which wasn't easy as they were kept in a box by the door of the tent.

"It says here," Algy sucked his cheeks, "you will either have an epiphany or a cathartic shock."

"Will it hurt?"

"Only if you go insane. Not much risk of that, old bean."

"I say not," and they both chortled at the ludicrousness of it.

In fact, Biggles was stark raving mad, and had been for as long as he had been flying. No one had been able to prove this of course, because he was a famous flying ace, in fact, he was the most famous flying ace, which meant his sanity and his reputation was protected by order of the War Office. Which certainly made it easy when picking up Wrens, as the rule of thumb is never argue with a mad person and you can't argue with a famous flying ace. Life was sweet.

"So, anything childhood epiphanies?"

"Is that like choir practice?" Biggles asked whistling between his teeth, a worried look passed across Biggles face as he remember what the choirmaster to do to the boys when no one was looking.

"No different epiphany," Algy bit on his pencil. "We want the other one."

"The one we don't know what it is?"

"Hmm, yes."

"What if I had an epiphany while I had choir practice - while I singing an epiphany?"

"Were you ever in choir?"

"No," Biggles lied.

"Ah. Biggles, you're not making this easy."

"I'm Biggles."

"Yes, and that does cover quite a bit doesn't it. Look old man, isn't there anything about your childhood, which I can put down on this blasted report. Anything that would look interesting, otherwise the jolly group captain will have me back in the trenches, and I'd rather avoid the whole lose-my-head-before-morning-tea-thing, if you know what I mean."

"But Algy, we don't have trenches anymore, this is Iraq. All we have here are targets."

"Targets?"

"Yes, jolly Mister Saddam and his donkeys. No end of Mister Saddams over here."

"I see your point." Algy looked at the ceiling, "I don't supposed you were frightened by a donkey when you were a child."

"No, I'm Biggles."

"Biggles has no fears?"

"Only that this war will be over before I can get in my plane again."

"Aha! So, for you to overcome your fears," Algy wrote excitedly, "it's necessary for you to go out and shoot Mister Saddam and his donkeys, and this is important for the war effort."

"I never thought about it that way before, I say Algy, you are clever."

"Well then, that's settled. Biggles I'm putting you back on active duty."

"Was I ever off?"

"Well no, but we must go through the forms, mustn't we?"

"Right ho, old bean. So, can I go and start flying again?"

"Don't see why not. It's for the War effort."

"Toodle-pip and what!" Biggles bounced out of his couch and paused by the door. "And can I shot down the German medical planes and blow up Iran?"

"Course you can," Algy nodded, "for the War effort."

The Intelligence of War

The ready room was filled with friendly banter and trouser bombs, as the airmen and officers waited for the pre-flight briefing, Biggles and Algy dashed around the room flicking scarfs at each other and playing hopscotch.

"Biggles you'll be flying the shuftie-kite for Scuds along the Tigris," Group Captain Wilkinson pointed his baton at Biggles. A shuftie-kite was a reconnaissance aircraft, and generally a mission least liked among the aircrews as they had to fly slow and it opened them up to ack-ack on a stupendous scale.

"Oh Bovril! Skipper, I can do better than that, I mean I'm Biggles after all," said Biggles swatting Algy with his scarf.

"Zip it Biggles," the Group Captain ordered. "The Air Marshal himself, personally requested your assignment."

"What? Really? Spiffing."

The Air Marshal hadn't requested it at all but it had the desired effect of shutting Biggles up, and in the back of Wilkinson's head was the possibility of Biggles getting shot down which was a result in itself. The other possibility of our hero getting killed wasn't a possibility since even the Group Captain knew Biggles was indestructible.

"You'll be flying the Slingsby T67 Firefly, debriefing at 0400 hours. Dismissed." The Group Captain smirked, pivoted on his heel and almost vaulted out the tent door.

"What? What?" Biggles blew through his moustache. "What did he say?"

Biggles sat annoyed in his Slingsby Firefly, a propeller driven monoplane on loan from the Royal Jordanian Air Force to the RAF for the war. It wasn't enough it was a monoplane with no armament, equipped with nothing more than a high definition camera in its belly and a sense of irony. It also had to have bright bumble bees stripes on its propeller and painted a hideous yellow lemon chiffon colour as part of its training role. It's gleaming yellow shell made it little more than a Cessna with a camera and as close to a sitting duck as was possible in contemporary air warfare.

In the blue sky it was more visible than an angry Zeppelin attempting to hide inside Westminster Abbey during the coronation of Queen Elizabeth II.

The Group Captain had pretty much said to the Iraqi pilots: "Here is Biggles – Shoot him down!"

Biggles was so annoyed he refused to put on a flight suit and was only wearing a jump suit without insignia to vent his passive aggression.

Nevertheless Biggles flew the Firefly with the deft agility of a dragon-fly on the village pond, humming along the Tigris taking holiday snaps of Marsh Arabs in their arched reed houses as hawks and wrens fought bitter battles in the reeds below. It was the sort of beautiful landscape where Gertrude Bell and T. E. Lawrence would have played tennis and dodged Bedouin bullets while excavating Hittite tombs under a dying sun.

Then over the radio came a strident voice came: "Firefly! Firefly! On your six! Bandit! Bandit!"

"Heard you the first time, old man," Biggles muttered into the radio, still disbelieving the immortal Biggles had been put in an airplane so poorly equipped that a bald goose would have had a better chance of survival, as he pulled the joystick sharply to the right. At that precise moment a Iraqi MIG-25 blew past Biggles' Firefly so fast it was like he was standing still and the enemy kills stickers on Biggles' window were ripped off. The MiG's pilot couldn't believe he had seen this bright yellow monoplane idling across the sands and blanked to come round for a second look, screaming across the desert floor in a fury of impeding destruction.

Earlier the MIG-25 had been been looking for targets when it came across a General Dynamics EF-111A Raven electronic warfare aircraft high in the sky and unloaded 3 missiles at it, this immediately alerted eight USAF F-15s at long range and the MIG was now eluding them in a race for the Iranian border. It was only luck it had come across Biggles, and only extraordinary luck the Raven had alerted Biggles in time, but it was Biggles' genius as a pilot that had saved his life.

"I haven't time for this Bumph!" Biggles dove down looking for a convenient hill to hide behind, when he spotted a ziggurat perched beside the Tigris that might just do for what he had in mind. He had to judge the air speed just right, so the MIG would fly past just as he was hidden by the monument, if he was a shade too fast or too slow the MIG would blow him out of the sky. Now while he had the speed exactly right, he hadn't taken into account a stand of palm trees blocking his path and he ended up hanging 20 feet above the ground with indeed a bump. The MIG screeched above just as the eight USAF F-15s appeared and gave the MIG pilot little choice but to flee over the border into Iran.

"They would never stand for this in Blighty!" Biggles blew

through his moustache. Now Biggles was very annoyed. It was not known how many aircraft Biggles had crashed over the years, it was probably in the millions, even the billions, but he was always in too foul a mood to fill out his log book after crashing that no record was ever kept except to his indignation. Biggles looked down and to his considerable surprise found a fleet of black limousines and drivers were sitting beneath him, this surprise was followed by the cocking of an army Kalashnikov rifles being pointed at him.

The Iraqi War, had ended as soon as the dust settled, and all that was left for the Coalition was to monitor the descent into hell of the Iraqi nation. Meanwhile, the Butcher of Baghdad was pacing back and forth deep down in his ziggurat, he had calculated the Coalition would expect him to use one of his million dollar concrete bomb proof bunkers to hide from their missiles, but he had out foxed them again, by running away and digging a cave complex under the most visible building for a hundred miles, he wasn't called the Wacky Iraqi for nothing. Who would think to find Saddam hiding under a rock in plain view.

Saddam was very pleased with himself, after all Saddam had done a much better job of conquering the Iraqi people than the American's could ever hope to do, and now they had failed to destroy him he knew he could legitimize his power if he waited long enough. Saddam was safe in his ziggurat as the Americans were searching for weapons of mass delusion, such as Scud missiles, desert submarines and the all important Iraqi Freedom of Disinformation Officer Mohammed Saeed al-Sahaf, better known as Baghdad Bob or Comical Ali, then Saddam had nothing to fear. Ali was famed for his relentless pursuit of the truth, no matter how many bombs were falling, the Iraqi doctor of spin could always make them miss. In fact, Ali was so tricky that before campaign he had disguised himself as an Italian prostitute and infiltrated the American's headquarters in Kuwait for two whole months, and while there he had not only foiled an assassination attempt on Saddam's life but had also acquired a considerable fortune from his expertise as a belly dancer. So Saddam not only had nothing to fear, he knew that one day he would return to power, drive the Americans and their British lapdogs from the holy Euphrates and kill even more Iraqis.

The sound of feet came running down the tunnel.

"Saddam! Saddam!" cried his intelligence officer.

Saddam pulled out a gold plated revolver and shot him.

"Yes?"

"We...capture a ... prisoner," intelligence officer number One gasped as he slumped to the ground.

Saddam shot him again and snorted, "That's for not having the intelligence to knock. Bring me the prisoner."

Biggles was hauled down the tunnel by intelligence officer number Two and thrown to Saddam's feet. It was not an auspicious start - thought Biggles.

"You spy?" a gold plated revolver lodged itself in Biggles' nasal cavity.

"Certainly not," Biggles wanted to sneeze but thought the gun might go off.

"You assassin?" the barrel twitched.

"I say rot to that, I'm an Englishman."

"Why you here?" the hammer cocked.

"Holidays?"

"Really?"

"Sure..."

"You funny guy. Welcome to Iraq." The characteristic grin of a tyrant in his element broke under Saddam's moustache as he holstered his pistol. "Iraq loves tourists, we have big industry, all for tourists."

"Thank you, pleased to be here," Biggles sighed in relief.

"Why you in jump suit?" The pistol lodged itself once more in Biggles' nose.

"Would you believe sky-diving?" Biggles eyebrows went super-orbital.

"During a war?" the hammer was recocked.

"It may be true, oh Sword of the Arabs!" said intelligence officer number Two with great enthusiasm, "His plane is painted yellow, it looks just like a skydiving plane, he has a parachute."

The gun went off. "Never interrupt your supreme leader," said Saddam, and intelligence officer number Three started edging to the door.

"What is your name?" the gun returned to Biggles' nose.

"Biggles."

"Biggles? Biggles? Is that a name?"

"Why certainly old bean, I'm the famous Biggles. Have you ever been to Kent?"

"Never heard of you, and I'm the famous Saddam Hussein Abd al-Majid al-Tikriti. President of the free republic, commander in chief of the armed forces, field marshal, the Struggler of Iraq, Standard Bearer, Knight of the Arab Nation, Sword of the Arabs, and prime minister of the all conquering Iraqi nation."

"Must be hell filling out a library card."

Saddam seemed satisfied and went back to pacing back and forth before the war maps.

"What are you doing? Old man," Biggles blew through his moustache.

"War, all is war, I am defeating those cowardly imperialist dogs who dare to invade my country, I will crush them into the sands, I will obliterate them from the sky, I will sink them beneath the seas. For I, Saddam, have never been defeated."

Intelligence Officer number Three had the presence of mind not to mention the first Iraq War.

"I, Saddam, have killed more infidels than Jimmy Carter has made Habitat Houses. I, Saddam, have burned the earth and annihilated the Persians. I, Saddam, have blasted Israel into oblivion. Here, have a cucumber sandwich, my mother makes them."

Biggles rolled his eyes and nibbled on hors-d'oeuvres, wondering at which point the mighty Saddam would explode from hubris or get to the point.

"I am planning my mighty attack on America," Saddam gestured grandly at a map of France, "My tanks will sweep down into New Jersey, my planes will bomb Chicago into rubble, my ships will blow San Francisco into confetti. That whore president Jimmy Carter will be ground into bones for daring to provoke the King of Babylon."

In truth, Saddam was a little behind the times, so his intelligence officer number Three coughed politely and pointed out George W. Bush was in fact the new president, and the third since Carter.

"What?" Saddam was too flabbergasted to shoot him. "Who gave the order for that?"

"Well, no one supreme lord of the desert, they voted him in."

"They can do that?"

"Yes," beads of sweat ran into intelligence officer number Three eyes, "grand mufti of the air, it's called democracy."

"Don't we have a democracy?"

"Yes, oh yes," intelligence officer number Three now sweated buckets, "oh juggernaut of destruction, however in our democracy only your supreme magnificence is allowed to vote."

Saddam turned to Biggles and smiled.

"See how superior Iraq is to the rest of the world. We first invented the one man democracy!"

Three hours later Saddam gave Biggles a bus ticket to Istanbul and told to come back anytime as Iraq needed its tourism, then shot intelligence officer number Three for daring to explain democracy to him.

In which Biggles is captured – yet again!

Biggles' plane came in too low; so low he accidentally landed on soccer field in the middle of a game, and was promptly arrested by the Iranian umpire for being offside.

The Iranian police captain sighed after Biggles had been arrested and held at the local station, "Can you tell me your name, please,"

"Shan't," said Biggles folding his arms across his chest defiantly.

The captain rubbed his forehead with both his hands, and sighed again.

"You're at least supposed to tell us your name, rank and serial number." He wearily explained for the ninth time. "As put down in the Geneva Convention on …"

"Shan't," Biggles poked out his tongue. "You jolly Saddams shot me down again."

The captain asked over his shoulder to another guard, "Is he talking about the foreign minister Saddam Saddam?" but the other guard shrugged his shoulders and continued drinking his tea.

"Look my name isn't Saddam," the captain began doodling on the paper, "my name is Captain Arash. I don't even know anyone called Saddam. I'm a Persian. Now for the love of God, can you please tell me your name?"

"What about the bally holes in my plane?" Biggles jabbed with his index finger on the table, "you can't get them fixed down the local bike shop you know!"

"You invade Iranian airspace, attack a field of sheep, and land in the middle of the quarter-final match between Iran and Kazakhstan of the Asia-Cup. Why shouldn't we shoot at your plane?"

"What about my cup of tea?" Biggles became petulant.

"It's right there in front of you, with milk even."

"Smell's like camel," Biggles poked his tongue at it.

"Yes," the captain rested his head on his hands and sighed with infinite patience "well, we couldn't get any milk from a Jersey cow as you requested, so we did the best we could and milked a donkey. It's perfectly good, although we do prefer only sugar and lemon with our tea."

"Any biscuits?"

The captain opened a box of Ferrero Rocher Chocolates.

"Will these do?"

"Ooh Ferrero-Rocher," Biggles grinned as he peeled one open.

"You're spoiling me."

"Look, someone from Savama," the captain almost pleaded with Biggles, "which is the Iranian Ministry of Intelligence and National Security will soon be here, and they torture people, so you're much better off telling me who you are or they might just tear it out of you."

"You cads!" shrieked Biggles, "I've been tortured by Russians, Italian waiters, French taxi drivers and even the occasional German High command - and trust me when it comes to being tortured the Huns know or two. Nobody tortures Biggles, ...oh bugger."

"Biggles," Captain Arash wrote this down, "with one or two 'g'?"

Biggles coughed embarrassed, "two."

"Rhymes with giggles?"

"You know, I've never noticed that before."

The captain looked at Biggles studiously for several minutes, trying to recall something, as Biggles face became more and more covered with chocolate.

"You're not the same Biggles we shot down a month ago, are you? The one who attacked a donkey and a field of sunflowers? The one who blew up Persepolis - one of our most treasured monuments, considered one of the great archaeological sites. The one who escaped by wearing a Burqa, after we had already handed him back to the British, so we had to hand him back twice? Not, that Biggles?"

Biggles' face went bright red and he looked awkwardly at the ceiling fan.

"No, that name is just a coincidence," Biggles lied unconvincingly. "Half the Royal Air Force is called Biggles. You're thinking of Rupert Biggles, I on the other hand am James Bigglesworth, different chap altogether."

"James Bigglesworth," the Captain wrote down meticulously.

"Oh bother!"

"And can you tell me why you invaded Iranian airspace?"

"Is this Iran?" Biggles looked startled. "I thought it was Egypt."

"Well, can you tell me why you invaded Egyptian airspace?"

"I thought it was on the way to Syria."

"And have you any reason for invading Syrian airspace."

"I was meeting a chap about a dog."

"So, let me get this straight, you were flying to Syria using a British Royal Air Force Harrier II attack jet," the captain looked sceptical, "armed with Air to Surface missiles and Paveway IV air burst bombs. Just to meet a man about a dog?"

"How on earth did you know all that?"

"Your logbook says," the Captain opened up a small notebook, "and I quote, 'fly Harrier II jump jet to Iran, and attack sheep with Air to Surface missiles and Paveway IV air burst bombs. Mister Saddam won't know what hit him. Be back in time for snooker with Algy and Ginger. I'm so spiffing. Biggles.'."

"If you bally well knew all this," Biggles looked annoyed, "why in blazes are you asking me?"

"When dealing with madmen, it pays to check your facts." The Captained smiled. "You're going to put into a hotel until such time as your government can explain why you are attacking all the sheep in my country."

"What about those jolly Savamas, the secret police chaps," Biggles quizzed worriedly, "the ones you said were going to torture me?"

"I just did," Captain Arash, grinned, "I actually am in the Savama. You see, Captain Biggles we're not idiots, my culture is over four thousand years old, it is comparable to Egypt, India and the ancient Greece. The Persian Empire was, and perhaps one day will be again, as complicated and vast as you could imagine. We are as sophisticated a people as you are ever likely to meet, and while the American press may seek to demonize us, a lot of us simply are not the monsters that we have been portrayed as, and though this may come as surprising to you – we do hold by the Geneva Convention, and you will in time be handed back to the British. We really couldn't do that, if you were in many pieces, now then could we?"

"Er, bally well say not." Biggles blew his cheeks out repeatedly.

"Except for one tiny little thing."

"Yes?"

"The chocolates were really laxatives. Good day."

Biggles Escapes!

For three days Biggles had wandered across the desert looking for rescue or at least a bus. It had gotten to the point where he wanted to be captured again. He had escaped from the Iranian secret police three nights before, by simply going outside for a cigarette, while they were watching some obscure Egyptian soap opera. The show was so incomprehensible it featured a young woman wearing nothing but a towel, who seemed to spend her entire life singing about a boy who had run off with a train driver. Biggles had gotten bored waiting for her to take off the towel. Since he could make neither head nor tail out of, he went for a walk, and after trudging over a sand dune to see what was on the other side; he had become completely and utterly lost. So out of sheer force of habit, he escaped and now he wanted to be caught again as that was his best chance to making it back to old Blighty.

At this moment, he was lying at the top of a sand dune watching a herd of sheep, and he was getting fed up with waiting to be captured. More to the point he wanted a good cup of tea, which was harder to find in this country than a man who wasn't wearing a dress.

"Oh, fiddlesticks," Biggles gave up and ran down the sand dune to the shepard waving his arms in the air and shouting hallo. The herdsman took one look at the stranger and began shooting at him. Biggles ran straight back up the dune and hid behind a rock. "I say," he said to himself, "what happened to the Geneva Convention?"

At the bottom of the hill, the sheep herder also hid behind a rock and for several minutes they cautiously watched each other. The herdsman was taking no chances, since over the last two weeks, strange planes had been coming out of nowhere strafing and bombing his herd and he was in no mood for idle conversation with foreigners.

"I say!" Biggles finally called out, "do you know the way to Piccadilly?"

The sharp retort of the rifle coincided with Biggles' flying cap being knocked off.

"I take it that's a no," Biggles picked up his cap and put it back on, to his annoyance he discovered the bullet had knocked off his Snoopy badge. He called out again from behind the rock. "By the way, I'm Biggles, so pleased to meet you."

The herdsman felt some confusion, as normally people always shot back at this point. A stranger stopping in the middle of the desert just for a conversation, either meant he was a cousin - and Biggles certainly didn't look like a cousin - or he was an enemy, and Biggles seemed too incompetent for either.

Maybe was he a rug salesman and a good rug salesman was hard to find.

"Hallo, foreigner!" he called out. "Have you carpets to sell?"

"Sorry Mister Saddam," Biggles called back jokingly, "I left them in the pick-up truck back in Sussex."

The herdsman, whose incredibly name really was Saddam, stood up and looked with surprise up the hill. He wondered how on earth the foreigner knew his name, and more to the point where was Sussex. Before too long Biggles was invited down to the camp for tea and sheep's eyeballs.

Biggles held one of the eyeballs up to his face.

"It's staring at me."

"That means it is happy to see you," laughed Saddam.

"What about the sheep?" Biggles was nervous.

"The sheep is not happy to see you," and Saddam clapped his hands at the absurdity of foreigners.

Biggles put it in his mouth and slowly bit down on it. It popped like a squishy sea polyp and burst open. He shuddered as he swallowed it.

"Rather tasty," he managed gasping, "I don't suppose you know where I could find a plane."

Saddam looked at him with some anger.

"There have been planes attacking my sheep," he picked up his old carbine, "do you know anything about this? I only have all these eyeballs, because I took them from the fly blown carcasses of all the dead ones."

Biggles gagged on the next eyeball.

"No, not a bit," he lied between retches, as he felt his taste buds turn into maggots "do you have any salt?"

The next day Saddam showed him how to ride camels and lead him across the desert. The Sun poured down upon the desert with such a villainous heat that at one Biggles point, in delirium thought he was playing County Cricket for Sheffield and would have taken the field to bat if Saddam hadn't kept dragging him back on the saddle. Crows circled in the sky cawing incessantly until Saddam shot one and gave it to Biggles for lunch.

"Aren't you having any?" asked Biggles as he poked at his fried crow.

"It is forbidden," grinned Saddam, "but it is not forbidden to serve it to unbelievers."

"Pretty sure they wouldn't serve this at Maxim's. It could do with a bottle of Chablis."

"Have you a wife, Biggles of the air?" asked Saddam.

"Yes, I call her Mrs. Biggles, I seem to have forgot her original name years ago."

"Is she as beautiful as a falcon soaring above an oasis?"

"More of a vulture hovering over a gasworks."

"These are things I know not of," muttered Saddam. "Is your country a great country?"

"Only when we beat the Australians at cricket," Biggles crunched down on a wing, "the rest of the time we have to explain the whole Empire thingy, and how the sun never sets - although of course it has, and continues to set with unfailing regularity."

"Strange is your world."

"Even stranger is your cooking."

"There is a hotel near here, where I am told there is good cooking."

"As long as the television doesn't show endless reruns of Egyptian soaps."

Which of course it did, being the same hotel he had absconded from four days beforehand. Oddly the Secret Police never noticed he was missing and were still watching the same obscure Egyptian soap opera - even odder still the girl was wearing the same towel and singing the same song about the train driver's boy.

Ace!

"Biggles, we are having trouble placing you, in fact your records seem to be out of date by a couple of decades. I'll need you to help me with the details."

"Yes sir," Biggles grinned then scratched his head, "Only to happy to oblige, will I need to contribute blood?"

"No, just your flying record and commissions, sorry but you seem to have fallen off the War Department radar and we need it for the regimental records."

"Yes sir, well, I started flying with the Royal Flying Corps in 1916 at seventeen years of age, actually I was twelve, but I just added a few years so I could join the rest of the squadron down the pub."

"Wait," the colonel blinked, "did you say 1916. That's ninety-four years ago."

"Yes sir, I keep trim by studying the ancient Tibetan art of drinking whiskey until four in the morning, for some reason, it's frozen my ageing process."

"I see," the colonel said slowly. "Starting with World War One then?"

"I seem to remember I flew an F.E.2, then a Sopwith Pup, then a Sopwith Camel and finally a Sopwith Elephant."

"Sorry," the Colonel looked up from his notes, "did you say Sopwith Elephant? I didn't know we had such an aircraft."

"Yes, it was an experimental flying tank," Biggles stroked his moustache as he remembered back, "looked like a giant hangar with wings but flew like a giant hangar with no wings - mostly downwards."

"And the Second World War?"

"Vickers Viking Mk 4, Supermarine S.6B, Spitfires, Hurricanes, Flying Fortresses, Shturmoviks, Yakovlev Yak-7, Messerschmitts, and Focke-Wulfs."

The colonel feverishly wrote all these down, and then looked wonderingly at Biggles, "You flew German planes?"

"I had a month's furlough, and the Group Captain said - 'don't come back until I had a fresh perspective'. So I took a fishing boat across the channel and joined the Luftwaffe, gives you no end of fresh perspective when you're looking down the sights of a plane which had previously been shooting at you."

"How many bogeys did you shot down?"

Biggles pulled out a handkerchief.

"Not boogies, I said bogeys!" The colonel yelled.

"Yes sir," Biggles grinned, "does that include all Boche, Frogs, Italians, Russkies, Turks, Swiss, Irish, Swedes, Armenians, Japs, Finns, Czechs, Poles, Cubans, Yanks, Mexicans, and English?"

"You shot down one of ours?"

"Only a couple of hundred and only when they crossed my line of fire," Biggles shrugged and gave his officially stupid look, "accidental and all that."

"Well, if you did in fact shoot any of those nationalities down, then I suppose yes."

"Do I include blimps, weather balloons, dirigibles, zeppelins, kites, sheep and seagulls?"

"Do you often shoot down seabirds?"

"I once read this book called Jonathan Livingston Seagull, and even since then I've had this unrelenting compulsion to blow them all to feathers and smithereens."

"In that case, no," the colonel sighed and rubbed his head, "just legitimate military targets."

"About eleven million, sir," Biggles stared at the ceiling in computation, "give or take three."

"Three million?"

"No, just three, I keep a running tally, I crossed the three million mark about an hour ago when I shot down a flock of Cessnas."

"Cessnas aren't military planes."

"Brazilian Air Force has some, well had some, now I expect they only have a navy."

"How do you keep a score of all these kills?"

"A portable abacus, sir," Biggles pulled out a folding abacus from his flying boot and showed it, "amazing little things."

Biggles commanding officer rubbed his temples and looked at Biggles as if he was something that shouldn't exist, this was so close to the truth that if he had known it would have bent reality around him.

"Biggles, are you sure this is all correct?"

"Yes sir, I'm British I can not lie."

"Hmm," the commanding officer thought little of this, "so, what fields of war have you engaged in?"

"Let's see," Biggles stared thoughtfully at the ceiling, "World War I of course, Turkish War of Independence; Third Anglo-Afghan War;

Great Arab Revolt in Palestine; World War II and all of it; Malayan Emergency; Korean War; Mau Mau Uprising; Suez Crisis; The Cod Wars with Iceland - I strafed a few sheep in that one; Dhofar Rebellion; Sealandic War of Independence – we lost that one to the damned Pirate radio station; Falklands War of course, more sheep strafing; Gulf War in Iraq – we won that one; Desert Fox War in Iraq; Kosovo War in Iraq; War in Afghanistan in Iraq, and of course the Iraq War in Iran."

"What?" the officer looked up in surprise, "The present war; here in Iraq?"

"No sir, the present Iraq war over there in Iran."

"But we're not at war with Iran."

"I had trouble with my GPS one day, just give me a theodolite and a compass I say, all this nonsense with satellites and what not."

"What happened?"

"I got lost and strafed some more sheep."

"So basically you're telling me you're over a hundred years old, you have flown every type of plane that has ever been made, and fought in every war the United Kingdom has ever been in."

"Yes sir," Biggles grinned happily, "that pretty well sums it up, except of course for the accident with the Time Machine."

The officer blinked slowly.

"Time machine?"

"Yes sir, at one point I was sent back in Time, hush-hush you know, with orders to kill Hitler."

"And you failed?"

"No sir, I accidentally invaded Poland and started World War Two, right cock up that one."

Biggles and the Undersand Railway

Biggles eventually escaped from the Iranian Secret police by standing outside his hotel and catching the nine o'clock bus to Tehran. He found himself sitting at the back of the bus, between a flock of goats and an enormous woman who ate nothing but fried chicken. To Biggles consternation, all of the buses' occupants -including the driver- spent the entire journey turned around in their seats, asking him about British soap operas, and most importantly the difference between Coronation and Ramsay Streets.

"But how can you people even have heard of Coronation Street?" Biggles shifted uncomfortably as chicken fat dripped on one shoulder and goats peed on the other.

"Coronation Street is the greatest art form that is exported to the Middle East," one learned bearded old woman explained.

"It is?" Biggles said more in amazement than inquiry. "Haven't you heard of Shakespeare?"

"Oh yes," she wheezed, "but only in Coronation Street are ugly old women portrayed in a noble way. Shakespeare makes them all in to …well ugly crones. Here in Iran, old women are now seen as interesting complex personalities. This is all due to Coronation Street."

"I never saw that one coming."

"Great art does that," she agreed.

Every few kilometres the bus driver would suddenly remember he was a bus driver, and wildly drag the steering wheel around to avoid hit the oncoming traffic, potholes, dead camels, low flying cruise missiles, and because it kept the bus going in a forward direction. This had the effect of turning the inside of the bus into the interior of a space ship re-entering orbit as chickens, goats and Biggles flew about in glorious abandon.

"Does he always drive like this?" Biggles grabbed an overhanging strap to stop being catapulted through the front window.

"How else could he drive?" came a hyperbolic reply.

"But isn't it dangerous?"

"More dangerous than if he didn't avoid crashing."

They stopped for a lunch break and fixed the axle, which had just fallen off. Biggles looked about the mountains that soared around him and wondered if this was near Kent.

"Cigarettes?" a voice floated at his elbow.

He looked down and to his surprise a man shuffling about on a cardboard mat, holding up a box of cigarettes. Both of his legs were missing and his face was horribly scarred from phosphorus burns, he looked like the victim of a napalm attack.

"What on Earth happened to you?" Biggles almost shrieked.

"War."

"You fought in the war?"

"No, I was late for work and got run over by a tank," the victim said sarcastically, "of course it was the war. Want to buy some cigarettes?"

"Which war?"

"Who cares which war, they're all the same."

"No, they're not," Biggles, insisted, "a war can be just, or unjust, moral or immoral. And there are the wars I fight on, the good ones."

"Look," the poor wretch wearily explained. "In war there four sides."

"Don't you mean two?"

"If you'd shut up, buy some cigarettes and let me explain."

"Oh right, um, lets say a pound?" Biggles handed over of the counterfeit Iranian Rials he had once dropped on a bombing round.

"In war," the victim explained, "there are four sides. The winners, the losers, the greedy blood sucking merchants and the victims, now guess which group I belong to?"

"Greedy blood sucking merchants?" Biggles erred on the side of caution as he lit up a Chesterfield.

"Do I look like a greedy blood sucking war merchant?" the cripple asked in amazement.

"Do cigarettes cause cancer?"

"Well, yes."

"Are you the result of a war?"

"Obviously."

"And did you just make a profit?"

"Only a tiny one," the veteran starred up with an angry look, "I have to eat and feed my wife and children."

"Ergo, you are a merchant of war," grinned Biggles and ran off before the cripple could bite his ankles.

"You feckin' English bastard!" was all the poor fellow could come up with, as he tried to drag himself after Biggles.

The bus journey had started again, once Biggles commandeered the bus driver's seat, by pointing out that as an ace pilot he could fly anything even a runaway bus, as he kicked the driver out the door, and tore off down the road with passengers and the driver in hot pursuit.

"It's a long way to Tipperary, It's a long way to go." Biggles merrily sang, "It's a long way to Tipperary. To the sweetest girl I know!" then he paused as he mentally calculated the distance to Tipperary.

"Hey," he said to himself. "It really is a long way to Tipperary."

He swerved the bus round and headed back towards Iraq and the officer's mess in Baghdad.

"Sorry" he called out as he roared past the passengers. "I'm late for snooker night."

Before disappearing in a storm of dust over the horizon. It all would have been another splendid escape - if he hadn't run out of diesel at the very hotel he had escaped from the day before.

Biggles in the Theatre of War

Most people of any magnitude, graduate from school with honours like magna cum laude and summa cum laud. In Biggles case, he had been ejected from Malton College public school as Corruptio Optimi Pessima, which roughly translates as most horrible of the finest. As a result, the best he could hope for was a position in a third world country as a doorstop, or he could hope for a state of continual world war and fortunately for him honour favours the insane and had been rewarded with a constant state of warfare since 1916.

He was in the medic tent with yet another part of his anatomy missing, having been hit by low flying anti-aircraft missiles, oddly this had occurred while playing snooker in the officer's tent. Since he attracted ack-ack in the same way Canadian geese attracted small pieces of lead whenever they flew over the American border, he put it down to an unusually enthusiastic Iranian gunnery sergeant.

"Blasted Saddam's!" he lay on his stomach clenching his teeth as the doctor probed his posterior with tweezers, "I was just about to make a break on the white ball and bam! I'm blown clean across the room and into the drinks cabinet. I wouldn't have minded so much, but Reggie owed me a fiver and he got blown to kingdom come."

"Please remain still, captain Bigglesworth," the doctor frowned as his tried to find the shrapnel in Biggles rear. "This is serious."

"So is a winning streak," Biggles went cross-eyed with a shot of pain, "What I'd like to know is how Jolly Saddam happened to put an ack-ack shell right in the officers tent, nine hundred miles from the front with Iran?"

"What front? No one told me about a front." The doctor looked up at Biggles with the sort of surprise a nurse has when she finds an elephant in the bedpan. He said holding up a shiny bit of metal with the tweezers. "But we're not at war with Iran. Are we?"

"Well, it's not so much we're at war with Iran, as I'm at war with Iran," Biggles whistled at a twinge, "according to the Geneva Convention, it only takes one side to declare war. So to speed things up I've declared war on Iran for the allies."

"Can you do that?"

"I'm Biggles you know." Biggles went cross-eyed with pain again, "Imagine World War I without a Bigglesworth. There see - you can't. That means I'm crucial for a state of war to exist. Hence, if anyone is going to declare war, it's jolly well going to be me."

"Not really surprising they're shooting at you while you're playing snooker," the doctor held a bandage to Biggles behind, "now then, is it?"

"Also dashed uncivilized, I would have thought."

"So is declaring war." The doctor grinned. "Now, don't sit down for a week."

"What do I do for pain killers?" Biggles would have whimpered but he was too heroic.

"A bottle of whiskey a day, or gin, whichever takes your fancy."

"I say," said Biggles, as he cheered up immensely, "this modern medicine has come a long way."

"No modern medicine is still in the Dark Ages, whereas the collectivized welfare state has created this instrument of torture for all doctors called the National Health Service, and they don't pay me enough to fill out a prescription for morphine. So you're bally well on your own captain Biggles. Now leave, your blood is congealing on the operating table and I want to clean it off."

Biggles blew through his moustache in irritation, but on reflection knew he was spending the next week in the officer's mess downing Singapore Slings and crooning Vera Lynn songs, until the hangovers drove him back to the indifferent arms of the National Health Service. So all things considered it was a boon for morale.

"Drink!" Biggles yelled at the adjutant behind the bar as he staggered in, "It's a medical emergency!"

"Biggles!" came a cheery voice out of nowhere.

"Spiffy!" Biggles yelled to his old flying chum, then leapt over the bar and tackled the barman as he was taking too long with his cocktail. "I thought you were blown up over Suez back in 56'."

"I was," Spiffy looked over the bar as Biggles started beating the adjutant to a pulp. "I've been a prisoner for the last fifty years in an Egyptian prisoner of war camp. I would have escaped but they have these amazing hummus dishes and endless Egyptian soap operas."

"I've watched some of those, incredibly boring I would have thought," Biggles grabbed a cocktail mixer and hammered it over the head of the adjutant. "When I yell for drink! I want a drink! It's a medical emergency!"

"Here Biggles," Spiffy poured a glass from his decanter. "Have one of mine."

"Oh Spiffy!" Biggles sighed happily and let the barman collapse to the floor, "You're a lifesaver. What are you flying now?"

"Tornados," Spiffy grinned and lit a cheroot, "got a mission tomorrow, all hush-hush you know."

"Splendid." Biggles downed half a pint of gin mixed with antifreeze. "Do tell."

"Can't old bean," Spiffy winked. "Mums the word."

"No Pims is the word, things have changed since you were last out." Biggles pulled out a service revolver and shot the adjutant in the leg. "And let that be a lesson!"

"Well in the case," Spiffy leaned over, "doing a recce over Tehran tomorrow."

"Will that be all, sir?" the adjutant held the blood back with a rag.

"Yes, and don't come back without a case of Boodles British Gin."

"Yes sir."

"And what's the box of ack-ack shells doing behind the bar, bally things could go off." Biggles turned back to Spiffy and resumed a conversation he had started fifty years before. "It's not like the Manfred von Richthofen is up and flying again, not after what I did to his …"

Outside the officer's mess Captain Arash of the Iranian secret service pulled out a wireless detonator from under his adjutant's cap and pulled the trigger. Ten seconds later Biggles landed in the infirmary, cradling a new war wound and screaming for a prescription for vodka.

Biggles and the Ziggurat

Biggles missed the aerodrome at Nasiriyah and landed his Harrier-jet on top of the Great Ziggurat of Ur. It was near a mistake, which anyone could have made provided they were blind drunk from a two-week bender at the Hotel Baghdad and hadn't accidentally stolen a jet fighter from the United States Marine Corps at Camp Adder. Biggles fell out of the cockpit and handed his car keys to a guide who came running up to remonstrate as this desecration of the ancient monument.

"And make sure you don't scratch the paintwork!" Biggles slurred, took three steps and collapsed in a puddle. He woke up the next morning surrounded by short men with large Kalashnikovs. They kicked him and yelled what he thought was something about no parking in Iraq. He lay on his back and wondered where he was, the guns weren't familiar, the men were certainly strangers, but the raging headache that was blocking out the sun was all too well known.

"Never again, oh crikey, never again," he moaned and threw up on the sandals of the leader of Al Queda in Iraq. The terrorists perceived this as a terrible insult and started wailing into his body with the butts of the rifles and kicking him repeatedly with vomit covered feet. None of which Biggles noticed as he was still wearing his flight helmet, blind drunk and a century of war wounds had left him immune to irony.

They hauled him to his feet and demanded to know his name.

"I'll take a Martini, preferably a Singapore sling followed by a saucy evening with Vera Lynn," he rolled his head and promptly threw up again on the chest of the leader. Once more they attacked him with fury that could only be matched by a stoic refusal on Biggles' part to sober up. Eventually they exhausted themselves and decided to hold him as either hostage, for ransom or at the very least for shooting practice. Remarkably they were able to disguise the Harrier-jet as a camel, and then dragged him away to a bunker in the base of the ziggurat.

Three days later Biggles finally sobered up staring up a bas-relief carving of the god king Hammurabi staring down at him.

"Wah!" Biggles shrieked, "I'm sorry headmaster but Jones made me do it!"

The noise brought the leader of the Al Queda troop swirling into the room in a flurry of robes. He stared down ferociously at Biggles who was pegged on with ropes on the floor. A short balding man with the intensity of a deranged otter, he had all the makings of someone with a future in self-exploding.

"I am Abu Abdullah al-Rashid al-Baghdadi," said the chief as coolly as he could muster, "leader of the Tanzim Qaidat al-Jihad fi Bilad al-Rafidayn."

"Tamzin," Biggles rolled his eyes. "Bit of a girls name, what?"

"Not Tamzin!" The leader shrieked, "I said Tanzim Qaidat al-Jihad fi Bilad al-Rafidayn."

"Like I said, Tamsin," Biggles stretched his jaw which Rashid had almost dislocated with a kick.

"I said Tanzim! Get it right!"

Biggles blew air through his moustache. "Only girls kick."

"We're not girls!"

"Tosh," Biggles grinned, "like your skirt, Tamsin."

"I'm not Tamsin!" Rashid completely lost his composure, "my name is Abu Abdullah al-Rashid al-Baghdadi, leader of the Tanzim Qaidat al-Jihad fi Bilad al-Rafidayn."

Biggles held his breath for a moment then giggled. "Still, you got to admit it does sound like Tamsin."

"You idiot!"

"Biggles to you."

"A-ha! You're the famous Biggles!"

"More famous than you are," Biggles grinned again.

This flustered Rashid completely. "Yes, but, no, but, …argh!" Then pulled out a revolver and started shooting wildly about the room. "Stop talking!"

Biggles went quiet but the grin on his face said everything.

"You are my prisoner!"

"Only because I'm tied up," Biggles snorted.

"That's the very definition of a prisoner!" Rashid went florid with rage. "You will obey my orders!"

"Tosh," Biggles looked sceptical, "that's what they said at Colditz and looked what happened there."

Rashid would have shot him but he had run out of bullets and stormed out of the room.

"You could at least offer me a cup of tea," Biggles shouted after him. "They did at Colditz!" Biggles returned to staring up at the carving of god king Hammurabi. "Haven't we met before?"

The floor was cold, hard and Biggles had a scratch between his legs that felt decidedly like it was moving. His eyes became round eyed and he tried to stare past his crotch at whatever was scratching his inner thigh. After a moment there was a scuttling and a giant camel-scorpion the size of a Fell terrier ran onto his chest and stared down at him with all the sympathy of a vulture sitting on an abattoir fence at offal hour.

"Shoo, shoo," Biggles tried to blow it away. "Go fetch."

The camel-scorpion rattled forward and stuck a hairy leg up Biggles' nose.

"Ooh, ugh," Biggles grimaced, at that moment Rashid came storming back in the room with a fully loaded pistol and the camel-scorpion ran off into the shadows. "Thank heavens you're back." Biggles breathed again.

"What?" Rashid looked startled at Biggles, not expecting a welcome and not seeing the spider. He was going to shoot Biggles, but now wasn't so sure as he pointed the gun at Biggles head. "You want me to shoot you?"

Biggles stared up at Rashid and wondered if this was part of some floor-show.

"We're not alone," Biggles whispered, and looked with his eyes at where the camel-scorpion was hiding.

Rashid looked about and seeing nothing but the statues, laughed at Biggles.

"Ha, you fear the ghost of Hammurabi!"

"No," Biggles sweated as he listened to the scuttling, "but I am worried about your terrier laying eggs in my nasal cavities."

"Bah," Rashid put away the pistol, "you speak madness, they must have left you in the sun too long." Then he pulled out a knife and cut the ropes on Biggles, setting him free. "It would be inhospitable to kill a madman."

"Whose mad?" Biggles jumped to the opposite side of the room of the scorpion. "You have a bug infestation that would rival the plagues of Egypt."

"Hmm," Rashid stroked his beard and looked thoughtful. "You are either brave or mad, I can not tell the difference."

"Trust me Tamsin," Biggles tried climbing up the statue. "It's not you I'm worried about."

"I said – Don't call me Tamsin!" Rashid yelled as he pulled out his pistol again. At that moment the giant camel scorpion ran out of the shadows. "Wah! A Djin!" Rashid dropped the pistol and clambered up the statue with Biggles. The scorpion hissed at them from the floor.

"Why are you up here?" Biggles yelled at Rashid. "This is your desert, you should be used to those things!"

"I'm from Cairo!" Rashid yelled back frantically, "I'm an art's student! Not a camel herder!"

There was a sickening crack as the statue they were hugging snapped free from the wall where it had remained for over two and half thousand years and fell like an mast to the desk with Biggles and Rashid riding it like damned sailors. They managed to roll free as the room exploded in a storm of flying rocks and dust, if a bomb had gone off they wouldn't have noticed it in the noise. They stood up and looked gingerly about the room.

"I think we killed it," said Rashid.

"I am Biggles you know," Biggles grinned. "That's what I do. I'm spiffying!"

The scorpion jumped on the fallen head of Hammurabi, its red eyes glowing in the gloom and raised its fangs like a toreador with his swords. The fangs were so large it made the Hound of the Baskervilles look like a rabbit with mange. With this apparition, any pretence of bravery fled the two and they fought each other up the stairs and raced off in opposite directions. Minutes later Biggles arrived back at Camp Adder with the Marine Corps Harrier-jet still camouflaged as a camel.

"Biggles," asked the group captain, "where in blazes have you been?"

"Sightseeing," Biggles said over his shoulder as he headed back to the officers regimental mess where he knew a supply of booze was hiding. "They have some amazing tourist attractions over here."

Biggles goes Ballistic

It was the desert war and Biggles buzzed the Shatt al-Arab waterway between Iran and Iraq. This was contrary to standard operating procedures that expressly forbid coming into contact the Iranians as that might start a small nuclear war, but Biggles kept giggling about the word "Shatt" in Shatt al-Arab and had to see for himself. Appropriately the "Shatt", as everyone in aerial command called it, was the arse end of the Tigris and Euphrates. Half a kilometre wide from Basra to the turquoise Arabian Gulf, it was the end result of 3,000 kilometres of open sewers and the run off from the oil fields, the natural border between Iran and Iraq and the scene of endless battles over the centuries. It was also Biggles playtime for that morning as he hunted for Scud missile launchers but he was happy to tank-knacker if he had the chance.

SAM missiles and ack-ack opened up on Biggles with glee abandon from both sides. Obviously the Iraqis didn't know Biggles was the greatest pilot since Pablo Picasso had the idea of strapping a small steam engine on a prostitute and bicycle before crashing off the Eiffel Tower in 1912, that wasn't art and wasn't aeronautics but was an amazing bit of piloting to watch. Meanwhile the SAM missiles went up as Biggles went down, the ack-ack exploded everywhere and Biggles was nowhere - Biggles was a ghost.

He flew past a giant poster on the Iranian side with the Supreme Leader of Iran Ali Khamenei shaking his fist at the west in his beard and robes and saying "America Can Do No Wrong." This translation was obviously mistake, but no one on the Western shore was bothering to telling the guys on the Eastern side. Biggles gleefully shook his fist back and was about to start whole World War III again, when a small pigeon flew straight into the cowling of his jet and did what the entire Iraqi army and airforce could not do, knocked him out of the sky.

"C of E!" Biggles yelped as his plane went into an uncontrollable spin, uncontrollable if you are not Biggles. Who despite seeing one whole wing explode into smithereens, the instrument panel do a saint Vitus dance and the avionics decide it was Belgium, was as cool as a cucumber sandwich on ice. Rather than banking left to compensate of the missing wing, he pulled full back on the remaining ailerons tilting the plane vertical and turned the entire craft into an enormous air-brake making a hundred meter standing stop. Then twisted the jet down flat like a cobra striking and pancaking on the water.

"Tickity-Boo!" Biggles grinned as the jet skidded up the river bank and crashed through the marshes. The moment he stopped the avionics computer came back online, recognized an impossible to recover stall at low altitude and automatically fired the ejector seat.

"Oh come on!" Biggles fumed as he shot up into the sky. The possibility of ejecting never even occurred to him till the parachute landed. "Bally things gone doolally!"

The marshes beneath stretched in a wide green belt from the river to the desert. Biggles could see in the distance palms, sand dunes and possibly a road which he made mental note of and checked his compass. As Biggles landed in the reeds herons squawked about him and tracer fire from the Iranian side blurred past. He knew it wouldn't be long before the Iraqis tried to grab him and use him for propaganda, so he ran off in the vague direction of west and kept his head down. After hours of struggling through duck nests, trampling on crocodiles, picking up water-borne parasites and generally doing all the tourists things he came to the first bit of dry land that was the Eastern edge of Iraq.

Just as he was about to light up a fag he heard the unmistakable sounds of Iraqi soldiers quietly trying to do sentry duty but failing terribly as it was like listening to the baggage train of the French army waltzing across Egypt during the Napoleonic wars. Cautiously Biggles poked his head above the reeds and to his surprise saw the opening to a concrete bunker not twenty feet in front of him, it looked suspiciously like the opening to a missile silo.

Saddam had the last remaining Scud missile, he was determined to destroy one of the American supercarriers in the Arabian Gulf, if only he could figure out how to fly it. The Scud had been earmarked for Iraq's moonshot ballistically this was impossible but you can go a long way in Iraq with imagination and a large budget. Instead the war happened and his engineers had come up with the amazing idea of putting a pilot in it to fly a suicide mission. It was intended the Scud would fly on autopilot to the last known position of the supercarrier and then the suicide jockey would take over when he saw the aircraft carrier screaming "I love Saddam!" as he buried its nose cone in the aft deck.

Unfortunately, there seemed to a lack of volunteers.

"What do you mean," screamed Saddam incensed beyond belief, "you can't find a good pilot? We are Iraq, we have the greatest pilots in the world, the largest navy, our army has never been defeated – how can you not find someone? I am Saddam Hussein Abd al-Majid al-Tikriti, lion of the desert, warrior of the sands, camel of the night! Of course my people want to die for me! I've killed enough of them, they should be used to it."

"But Saddam," his chief engineer of public sewage works and intercontinental missile development pleaded, "all our pilots have run away to Iran or been shot down."

"How hard can it be to fly?" the lion of the desert held a rifle to the engineer's head as a sign of paternal affection. "It's a rocket."

"It has never been done before, only our top test pilot could hope to succeed."

"And where is he?"

"The last we heard he was in a MIG fighter headed to Brazil."

"Brazil?"

"They have no extradition and have awesome Samba nights."

"Find me a pilot," the camel of the night growled, "or fly it yourself."

Meanwhile above the bunker, Biggles was reconnoitring to find out what the silo was for, this was the sort of intelligence that paid top money from the spivs in MI6. It paid so well that Biggles had once furnished a villa in Spain with titbits he had sold to British military intelligence during the War.

The base had been cleverly hidden in the mashes near the Arabian Gulf putting any ships well within range of the Al-Hussein Scud-B missile, appearing halfway between an oil refinery and a bird watchers hide, it clearly wasn't cleverly hidden at all, but in the mind of the great dictator of Babylon it was the perfect disguise. Biggles watched as the guards hunkered down over cups of teas and rice, their uniforms were in rags, their shoes falling apart but they had that eternal optimism of not wanting to be shot by Saddam so they didn't mind. He thought it was strange the rusty pumps and oil refining equipment didn't quite seem to match their purpose, then he realized they were dozens of camouflaged ack-ack guns and SAM missiles, and had probably been those responsible for shooting at Biggles.

On the path, in front of Biggles as he peered out from the reeds, appeared a soldier carrying a chamber pot. In his haste to serve his master and build the rocket the chief engineer of public sewage works and intercontinental missile development had neglected to install lavatories. The soldier idly spat and threw the contents of the chamber pot near

Biggles' hiding spot, this was too much for the man who had once introduced toilet paper to the Indian subcontinent, Biggles exploded out from the reeds and with a splendid punch on the jaw knocked the fellow clean out.

"Blighter!" Biggles hopped around on the spot cradling his hand, Biggles who had once boxed at the 1936 Olympic games and won several gold medals in a crooked poker game from Willy Kaiser had apparently had forgotten to close his fist. Once the pain stopped, Biggles stuck the chamber pot on the soldier's head and dragged him back into the reeds. This was followed with some earnest fumbling in the marsh until Biggles remembered he only wanted the fellow's clothes and dressed himself as an Iraqi soldier. Biggles wandered around the camp and every time he met someone he made a hacking noise with his throat that sounded like a dying camel, this brought a sense of bewilderment among the troops who told him to go to the doctor and get a prescription.

Eventually Biggles found the front door and waltzed like it was the presentation of débutantes at the start of the British social season.

"Toodle pip!" Biggles punched out half a dozen of Saddam's elite Republican guard before they had woken up from their afternoon snooze. Just as he finished a colonel in the Republican guard entered the room and looked at all the down soldiers.

"They were sleeping on the job, sir," Biggles giggled and saluted.

"Well done soldier, you're now a sergeant." The colonel saluted back, "take some stripes and report to the brigadier down stairs."

"Yes sir!"

Biggles ran down stairs and punched out the first captain he saw, threw him over his shoulder and ran down another flight of stairs. He dumped the body at the feet of the brigadier.

"Sir! I captured a spy!" Biggles giggled and saluted.

"My nephew is a spy?" The brigadier was amazed.

"Yes sir, selling secrets to the enemy."

"And I went to his wedding," the brigadier returned the salute, "take his bars you're now a captain and report down stairs. Wait, why are you speaking English?"

"For the emperor!" Biggles giggled, punched out the brigadier and took his jacket.

On the next floor he ran into Saddam.

Saddam marched back and forth, a gun in either hand, he had

grown paranoid in the last few decades and was prone to putting holes in shadows and ministers of state. He felt the responsibility of command on his shoulders, for he and only he could lead his people to triumph, his descendants would sing paeans of his victories over the dog Americans and their lapdogs the English. If only his troops would stop running away every time a stray dog barked. At one point Saddam had thought of dressing up all the goats in his country since his own troops kept running away to sham them into victory, but the test goats being goats they ate the test uniforms so Saddam ate them.

Medically he was a wreck, and since the bombs had started raining down he had these terrible headaches, he tried codeine, morphine, benzodiazepine but nothing stopped the bombs falling. What was worse was the nightmares, those shivering terrors at three o'clock in the afternoon after his Pilates classes. They were waking nightmares where he looked at photos of all the massacres he had perpetrated and wondered if he could have done better. He had shot four of his personal physicians but that didn't seem to make him better either. If he didn't find a solution to this war he would be dead before his time.

Then Biggles marched in and saluted, quite possibly the best looking Iraqi soldier Saddam had ever seen, and for a moment Saddam was jealous enough to consider shooting him.

"A volunteer! My boy, my son!" and kissed him on both cheeks. "What you do will save our people!"

Biggles considered kneeing him in return but with Saddam's twenty actual sons were all holding gold plated Kalashnikovs in a circle around him, Biggles didn't fancy his chances.

"And you are willing to crush our enemies and live in the hearts of the Iraqi nation forever?"

Biggles had no idea what was being said, so he nodded his head vigorously.

Saddam held him close and peered in his eyes.

"You don't look local," Saddam said suspiciously, "are you Circassian?"

Again Biggles nodded without conviction.

"Excellent!" Saddam was satisfied, "see everyone, even foreigners wish to die for me! Report to the hanger deck! You are our new astronaut!"

Biggles found himself strapped into a cockpit that had the sort of guidance system that would grow hair on a duck, its wiring grew profusely out of cardboard boxes, its controls and buttons made of fairy lights and Lego blocks. The smell of burning plastic perfused the cabin, the popping of telephone exchange gearing went off continually. It was the sort of Heath Robinson affair that would have given Wernher von Braun a stroke. The Al-Hussein Scud-B missile like its namesake was not a clever weapon, it was not well made and at the best of times tended to explode the moment the ignition was pushed.

"I say old man," Biggles looked at the chief engineer, "you sure you know what you're doing?"

"I work for Saddam, I had better," said Iraq's chief rocket specialist with the toothless grin of a goatherd.

"And this thing will fly?"

"It has an engine."

"That's not what I asked." Biggles furrowed his brow, "what's with all the Meccano, Erector set and string?"

"Wartime shortages," the chief engineer smacked Biggles' hand, "don't push that button."

"Why, what happens if I push that button?"

"Glorious victory!"

"I wasn't worried before but now I am."

It had a joystick, and that was all Biggles really needed to know.

"Where are the pedals?"

"Removed to save weight."

"So why am I sitting on bricks?"

"We couldn't afford an ejector seat."

"You really have thought of everything."

"You take off in two minutes, any last words?"

"Only that I'm amazing." Biggles truly was amazing as twenty minutes later he became the first and only person to land a Scud missile on the deck of an aircraft carrier.

Biggles Defeats the Desert

Biggles was lost; he had been lost from the moment he had taken off from Forward Operating Base Falcon, this mainly due to his taking a cup of tea into the cockpit and spilling it on the navcom computer, not only destroying a thirty thousand pound computer, making all communications and navigation impossible but also ruining his morning cuppa.

He had been flying for almost three days now, busily refuelling in mid-air each time his fuel gauge fell to empty. He achieved this by mugging any passing U.S. KC-135 Stratotankers. It was a mugging because he would shoot across their nose-cones until they gave into his demand for extra fuel, and the fact they refused to offer him tea and crumpet was starting to annoy him. Four times the U.S.A.A.F had launched intercept squadrons to shoot him down for piracy, but each time he had given them the slip but flying upside down into a dust storm, he was after all Biggles.

"Jolly ho," Biggles said to the ghosts of all the pilots he had flown with, "I could do with a nap."

It was not unknown for Biggles to fly in his sleep. For any other aeronaut this would be considered impossible, but Biggles had a brain the size of a finch and like a finch could sleep on the wing. Five minutes after falling asleep he crashed into a sand dune in the middle of the great desert. He might be able to fly asleep, but his plane still needed fuel to fly.

He woke up wrapped in a parachute and wondered if this was the Savoy, tried to fluff his pillows and promptly went back to sleep. The ejection seat had fired automatically when he clipped the leading edge of a sand dune and fired him fifty feet straight up and down onto the trailing side of the dune. The fighter jet had smacked incontrovertibly into a stand of date trees and exploded.

The next day Biggles woken and tried to ring for room service, this was of course impossible, but everything about Biggles was impossible so was in no way the unexpected. What was unexpected was the sudden appearance of a Bedouin shepherd offering him a cup of coffee.

The Bedouin had their camp at the base of the sand dune and had woken in the middle of the night to a tremendous crash as Biggles' plane had wiped out their only stand of date trees for fifty miles in any direction. Since this was their only source of revenue besides hostage taking, they were sorely put out, but the requirements of hospitality in the desert forced them to take care of any lost strangers until they had a reason to cut his throat or sell him for a camel in the nearest village.

Biggles blinked and stretched, took the coffee without thought and asked for some crumpet.

"No English," said the chief of the Bedouin sizing up the pilot, "we have no crumpet. We only have dates and camel's milk. But no crumpet, I am very sorry. Are you rich?"

"Why is there so much sand in the Savoy Hotel?" Biggles said, still waking up. "I know the Saudis own it, but there's really no need to fill it with Saudi Arabia, is there old bean?"

The chief looked around and wondered what the stranger was talking about.

"Savoy?" he asked as the wind whipped particles of sand into his face.

"Ah," Biggles gave him back the coffee cup, undid his harness and stood up. "This isn't the Savoy Hotel, is it?"

"No English, this is the Nefud, the great desert of Arabia."

"So, definitely no crumpet then?"

"Not unless you are very rich."

"And if I was very rich?"

"Then I would ransom you for much gold and buy you all the crumpets you desire."

"And if I'm poor?"

"Then either I will cut your throat or sell you for a camel at the great camel market."

"When in that case, I'm loaded," Biggles grinned weakly.

"That is very good to hear English," the Bedouin sheikh had finished sizing him up and made a decision not to murder Biggles, at least not until a ransom had been paid. "You will be my guest for the present. I ask only that you respect our customs and do not attempt to escape."

"What are your customs?"

"Leave our women alone and don't molest the donkeys."

"Do people often molest your donkeys?"

"More often than they molest our women" the sheikh grinned.

At the camp Biggles was introduced to a family so extended it started in Damascus and ended in Detroit, most weren't immediately available but they were mentioned in passing and deed.

"And finally I mention my ninety-seventh cousin Ali ben Rahsid ben Sali, who drives a taxi in Tierra del Fuego."

Biggles eyes had long glazed over and was surprised the sun was still shinning as they sat in the black tent of his host.

"Really," he blinked himself awake, "you don't say."

"And yourself, English, tell me of your family."

Biggles blew air through his moustache and looked thoughtful.

"Hmm, well let's see. There's my grand aunt Olga Von Bigglesbottom, she got arrested for selling official secrets to Stalin back during the cold war. Although fair's fair I say, I can't see how the catcher chute on a combine-harvester falls within the purview of the Official Secrets Act. She's been on the run for sixty years now, and given the fact no one has seen her for the last fifty, and the fact she must over one hundred and forty years old now, might actually mean she is dead, but who knows. I mean any woman who has slept with every leader from Neville Chamberlain to Pol Pot is capable of anything I say."

"I see," the sheikh said to be polite.

"Then there's grand uncle Rupert del Biggles-Smyth-Oppenheimer who once tried to sell the Eyrie Canal back to the Americans shortly after they constructed it. Would have succeeded too - if they hadn't noticed this new canal wasn't in California like he said. He is at present serving a three thousand year sentence for defrauding the Crown over a counterfeit barge tax, which was supposed to charge a guinea to everyone on a canal who wasn't wear a tartan kilt. Obsessed with inland waterways, he is."

"Err," the sheikh would have looked at a watch if he had one. "Interesting."

"Next comes my great-great nephew Dagmar Erskin-Biggles, last of the great explorers. He started exploring at the ripe old age of six weeks when he escaped from his crib in Wellington Barracks and ended up on a safari in Zululand shooting gazelles for his royal highness Goodwill Zwelithini kaBhekuzulu." Biggles looked wistful. "They grow up so fast these days."

The Bedouin sheikh rubbed his forehead.

"I should also mention my great cousin Peter Alexeyevich Biggles-Kropotkin a biologist who specialized in the scatology of Coleoptera and overthrowing the Tzarsist state... he has a very interesting career..."

It was in the vein Biggles kept talking for a week, until he woke up one morning and found the camp deserted with a letter pinned to his flight suit suggesting he take the next bus back to England.

Biggles and the War of the Hummus

Biggles had landed in Israel, it wasn't intentional but he had a bet with Algy that hummus had paprika in it, and given that Israel was the largest producer of hummus in the Middle East he promptly flew over the Iraq border to see for himself. He landed in the Golan Heights and was shot at from both sides. The Syrians fired at him because he had flown over their country, and the Israelis launched anti-air missiles because sixty years of neighbourly aggression has made them awfully trigger-happy.

A jeep screamed to a halt and a short angry man wearing an enormous camouflage shower cap leapt out and started screaming at Biggles. Our hero was still sitting in his cockpit with a bemused expression on his face. His plane was broken in two, the wings had been torn off and the plane was riddled with bullet holes. Biggles had only survived by being amazing. The screaming continued for several minutes, until it transpired the solider was merely asking for identity papers.

"Why do you have a shower cap on your head?" Biggles was mystified at the odd shape on the soldier's head, as he stepped free from what was left of his Harrier jump jet.

"What?" the Israeli solider said in equal surprise.

Biggles pointed at the amorphous hat on the soldier's helmet.

"This?" the solider looked up from the papers, then started shouting in Israeli for several minutes before quietly replying in English. "This is a mitznefet, it is camouflage netting, it breaks up the shape of the head, makes us hard see."

"Looks like a chef's hat," Biggles giggled.

Again the yelling started again, Hebrew was the only language where the vowels ganged up together and beat the crap out consonants, then the soldier dropped back to English. "You have invaded Israeli airspace, you must come with me."

"Is there paprika in hummus?" Biggles said obliquely.

The yelling began again in a language so old its grammar had rigor mortis, followed by a more restrained: "Sometimes. Yes, a lot of Hungarians put paprika in their hummus. They're a few restaurants in the city of Tel Aviv which sell it, but enough of this - you are under arrest, please come with me."

"Television, righty-ho," said Biggles and walked around to what he imagined was the passenger side, got in and in a pique of absentmindedness drove off.

From behind him a torrent of Yiddish insults exploded, followed by a more sedate rattling of a Tavor assault rifle puncturing 5.56 mm holes in the back of the jeep.

"Now about hummus," Biggles started driving towards the Mediterranean. "I think this Television City is the place to go."

Biggles drove down the Golan Heights noting the ruins of thousands of tanks and endless olive groves. It was a countryside that had seen so much history it was now layered down as geological strata. It had witnessed the boots of many hordes of conquering armies of history, from Babylonians to Egyptians, Hittites to Romans, Crusaders to Mongols. Yet it is a surprising footnote in history, that if you actually counted the number and types of boots that had walked this desert, then most of them were recently manufactured in California and belonged to American tourists with names like Shirley or Bob.

He drove straight into Israeli because no one questioned an Israeli jeep, and he kept talking about hummus to the border guards till they waved him on in desperation. The countryside was dressed in its gentle green spring colours, filled with the delightful scent of jasmine and cordite. It was this year's bi-annual Arab uprising, and Hezbollah had managed to sneak a submarine into the Sea of Galilee. Rockets were being from the nearby sea, as Hezbollah fought a hit and dive campaign that was confusing the crap out the Israeli Defence Force. The IDF had neglected to park a destroyer in the inland sea and were scratching their heads on this one.

Biggles watched as another errant missile passed close overhead and destroyed a nearby haystack. Hezbollah were huge on imagination but appalling on fire control. They had destroyed nineteen haystacks that morning, were reporting the Jihad had conquered Israel and already driven the Hebrews back into Egypt. Did I mention they were huge on imagination?

He drove in a small hamlet that turned out to be a hidden military base in a kibbutz. Again no one stopped him, as everyone in a flight suit looks the same, or assumed he was on special assignment from the RAF, until he walked into the mess and asked about where the nearest television station was meant to be and did they have any Hungarian hummus.

Nine short men armed with Tavor assault rifles dragged him under a bench to shelter from the missiles. They began yelling with enthusiastic anger at their mother's cooking, the price of imported white goods, and how much their feet hurt. It was sometime before they actually spoke in a language that didn't try to strangle the speaker's oesophagus on the way out.

"I'm looking for the television station," Biggles insisted. "They have restaurants that sell Hungarian hummus. I've got a bet with Algy the stuff exists. Although really, I am Biggles, you'd think that was spiffy enough to prove any wager."

There was the whine and crash as yet another sea-to-haystack missile landed nowhere nearby.

"You mean Tel Aviv?" asked the captain of the commandos, as plaster fell from the ceiling.

"Does it have hummus?"

"Is the sky blue?"

"Why do you want Hungarian hummus?"

"It's for a bet. Algy says hummus has paprika in it."

"Well yes, of course hummus has paprika in it."

"Yuck I hate paprika. Who is shooting at you?"

"Hezbollah, they don't like us."

"Have you tried giving them your cooking?"

"Will that work?"

"At the present moment in time you've got nothing to lose." Another bomb went off, and another haystack exploded. "Why do your haystacks keep exploding?"

"We've hidden fake radar transmitters in them, the rockets are trying to take out our actual radar but they are tricked into bombing the wrong targets."

"Clever."

"Yes," grinned the commando, "we're not Israelis for nothing. Did they shoot down your plane?"

"Shot down?" Biggles laughed off the possibility, over the years Biggles had been shot down so many times he now regarded the whole process as nothing more than a bumpy landing, "Biggles doesn't get shot down, I use everything as a landing strip." The thump of another haystack sounded near. "Why don't your rockets fire back at them?"

"They made a submarine in the Sea of Galilee," the commando shrugged, "we're having trouble tracking them down."

"The rotters!"

"I know," the commando grinned, taking to this mad Englishman. "Look can I help you? The British consulate maybe?"

"Is there an airbase nearby?" Biggles' eyes were forever on the sky.

"Well, there is the Ramat David Air Force Base, that's not too far away. I expect you need to report in."

"I remember Ramat," Biggles perked up, "Roald Dahl and I used to fly Hawker Hurricanes out of Ramat during the war with the Bosch. Odd, I'd forgotten I'd been here before. I defeated Rommel you know."

"In that case," the commando started laughing, not knowing Biggles was completely serious, "we really must get you to Ramat."

An hour later at Ramat a dusty Biggles borrowed a de Havilland DH.82 Tiger Moth used for training out from under the eyes of the instructor. Biggles loaded it up with bottles of hummus - without paprika just to prove a point to Algy, and took off before the air traffic control had realized he was even on the tarmac.

Biggles was now in control of a WWI aircraft that had so little a radar signature that they thought he was a flock of geese migrating. A very erratic flock of geese as he wove and ducked about the sky trying to find one of those damned Bosch. This didn't prevent a F-16 chase plane being sent up after him once they discovered a missing plane, however, Biggles was so erratic and the jet was so fast the Israeli pilot repeatedly overflew our hero.

It wasn't long before he was flying low over the Sea of Galilee, and just as he inverted he passed over the submarine that had been bombing him before, a bottle of hummus fell out of the cockpit and straight down the conning tower of the submarine and landed inside with a shattering crash. This event was coincidental with the F-16 screeching past as it broke the sound barrier and banking back into Israeli airspace. The combination of being bombed with hummus and buzzed by the air force was too much for the insurgents who fled the submarine. The matter was brought up next day in the United Nations that bombing people with hummus was as a crime against humanity and could they have their submarine back.

Biggles landed back in the American air force base at Camp Liberty in Iraq and showed Algy the hummus.

"Not hummus," Algy laughed, "I said Hummers. I said American Hummers have power steering."

Biggles and the Tiger

Biggles crossed the great divide and flew into the unknown, or as was more commonly known - he broke into the Women's Auxiliary Air Force dorm with a bottle of Irish whisky and an inclination that couldn't be scratched. He was cornered in an airing closet by major Daphne Bodice-Splitter whose double-barrelled name was the stuff of legends.

"Captain Biggles!" she yelled as she surrounded him with two signals WAAFs armed with fire extinguishers. "Put down lieutenant Higginbottom, she's on active duty!"

Biggles and Higginbottom collapsed in a puddle on the floor. Higginbottom tried to salute but her hand was caught in Biggles' flight suit and Biggles was upside down. Biggles tried to stand up but couldn't decide which direction that was and kept sticking his head in a basket of unwashed nether garments and only succeeded in covering his head in stockings and bras. Eventually they righted him, sat him on a stool and demanded he explain his actions.

"Isn't this Bomber Command?" he looked about in drunken perplexity. "Could have sworn I had a pre-flight briefing here today."

"The only briefs are on your head!" Daphne snapped.

"Odd looking oxygen mask," he held it up. Daphne grabbed one of the fire extinguishers and hosed him down. "Crickey! It's Flak!"

"Captain Biggles explain yourself or I will call the sergeant-at-arms!" It was three in the morning and major Daphne Bodice-Splitter was dressed in a terry-towelling ensemble that left everything to the imagination. She was in no mood for drunken airmen fossicking in her ironing room, and if he weren't the famous Biggles she would have shot him.

Blearily Biggles waved his arms around and tried to hold the room up.

"It's like this," he said and gave a three minute incoherent ramble about Mussolini not returning his dress suit back in 43', after he had had parachuted out over Rome during a failed bombing run and gotten lost in the Colosseum for a week, finishing with, "…it's nothing like Three Coins in a Fountain with Audrey Hepburn – Audrey!" he shrieked out.

Daphne blinked several times and ordered him thrown out a window. Biggles landed in a flowerbed before wandering off through the night haranguing several stop signs he met on the way.

He woke up in the morning with an Iraqi gardener poking him with a rake. The sun was shining, the air was crisp with sand and Biggles had a headache that could have threatened world peace if it ever escaped the confines of his ever-shrinking brain.

"English," the Iraqi gardener poked him again with the rake, "are you ill?"

"Never better," Biggles stood to his feet and promptly fell over, this was followed by a brief ejaculation of vomit. Once this subsided, he stood up again and gave his credentials. "I'm an officer in the Royal Air Force, this is how we normally wake up in the morning. Where am I?"

"Baghdad Zoo," the gardener returned to sweeping bomb fragments. "You are in the tiger enclosure."

Biggles found three Bengali tigers staring intently at him from shadows, he also found he was locked in the cage with them.

"I don't suppose you could let me out?" Biggles rattled the cage like a disgruntled baboon.

"That is up to the judge who put you there," the sweeping continued.

"Why would he put me in the tiger enclosure?" Biggles rolled his eyes in amazement, "I mean, I am Biggles after all."

"We can no longer afford prisons, every time we build one, either the Americans blow it up try to blow up Al-Qaeda, or Al-Qaeda blows it up trying to blow up the Americans. You may have noticed there has recently been a great deal of blowing up in Iraq."

"What about the tigers?"

"They are all suffering from Post Traumatic Stress Syndrome from all the explosions and are too afraid to do anything," then the gardener grinned, "Also they save on prison guards."

"And why am I in here?" Biggles scratched his head and looked for fleas.

"English, I was told you were caught pissing in the Tigris. Ironic is it not, from Tigris to Tigers."

"Have you seen how polluted the Tigris is?"

"That is why we have so many laws against pissing in it."

Biggles spent the morning grooming a five hundred pound Bengal tiger until the provost marshal arrived to investigate the charges.

"It says here," the provost marshal flipped through a clipboard, "you not only tried to steal a milk float, but you also drove it at high speed through the streets of Baghdad screaming Marco Polo, Marco Polo, defying anyone to cross the street and pelting the residents with ice slurpies and frozen yogurt."

"Must have been a good night, jolly what?"

"Yes, indeed," the provost marshal wrote this down, "have you any defence?"

"I have no memory of any of this."

"No memory," the provost marshal sighed, "care to make a statement?"

"I'm British."

"That's your statement?"

"It says it all."

"Wouldn't care to elaborate?"

"Where would the world be without cricket?"

The provost marshal took a deep breath. "Alright, since no witnesses are willing to testify, as witnesses have a tendency to disappear if they do, and since you have memory of anything, I'm forced to let you go."

"Can I take Riley with me?" Biggles pointed at the giant tiger purring next to him.

"Don't see why not, not on the clipboard."

"Jolly!" Biggles was ecstatic, "if this doesn't put me in the good books with WAAFs then nothing will."

The look on the tiger could only be described as startled.

Biggles and the Nightmare

Biggles woke at three in the afternoon and wondered if his bed was on fire. After a moment's reflection he accepted it was, grabbed a box of cigars and jumped out the window.

"Fire!" he screamed and immediately a howitzer stationed beneath his Nissen hut opened fired and destroyed the local water works. Biggles had fallen asleep with a box of Havanas and set fire to his room, it was only a ferret-like instinct for survival and the fact he always slept with an open window insured his continued existence. It was the fifth Nissen hut he had burned down that month and sleepily wondered if smoking really was unhealthy.

"Biggles!" Group Captain Wilkinson stared down at Biggles lying in the sand. Biggles was cradling a box of Cubans, his teddy bear and trying to get back to sleep. "Report for briefing."

"Not now matron," Biggles smiled as he fell asleep, "in the morning, and biscuits please."

"Biggles!" Wilkinson kicked Biggles feet. "Report for briefing, or I'll have you shot for insubordination!"

"Not the whip matron!" Biggles blurted out in his sleep. "Not the whip!"

Five minutes later he staggered into briefing tent with a cup of tea, his teddy and dragging a sleeping bag he had pilfered. He collapsed at a desk and laid his head on the bear. Ten seconds later a five-foot ruler crashed down next to his face and he woke up with a jolt.

"So glad you could join us Captain Biggles!" Group Captain Wilkinson yelled at him.

"Ginger!" he yelped and rolled his eyes around, trying to get his bearings. "Jerry's on your tail!"

Biggles had been now awake for three days, after a reconnaissance mission over the southern Zagros Mountains had gone terribly awry and he had landed his Hawker GR-9 Jump Jet in the main Bazaar of Istanbul. How he had flown off course by 1500 miles was a matter of some confusion, but was probably due to his the teddy bear instead of the navigation computer for directions. After being chased by the Turkish Secret Police, through most of the streets in Istanbul, Biggles had finally escaped into the largest brothel this side of the Cairo and suffered a worse case of sleep deprivation than the secret police could have ever achieved. Three days later, it had taken five burly Royal marines in the middle of the night to drag him away from the intoxicating rhythms of a room filled with Turkish belly dancers and Irish whisky.

Group Captain Wilkinson resumed his position at the front of the room.

"Thanks to Captain Biggles' unfailing ability to lose the recon photos of the Iranian base at Imam Ali, near Khoramabad in the Zagros Mountains, we are forced to repeat the mission." He pointed at a map with a laser. "Now we know the Iranians are up to something, because Khoramabad had the word 'bad' in it. Or at least this is what MI-7 has decided, and given MI-7 is the propaganda division of military intelligence – their opinion may be subject to interpretation. So we are forced to undertake the mission, yet again. Any questions?"

Biggles sat up and stared about the room blearily. It was at this point he realized he was the only person in the room beside Group Captain Wilkinson. He frowned. This meant he was going to take the mission. Then he smiled and wondered how long it would take to get back to Istanbul.

"Any volunteers?" Group Captain Wilkinson stared Biggles.

Biggles grinned, thought about the brothel he was about to elope to and held up a flying glove. "When Blighty calls – I'll be there!"

Group Captain Wilkinson smiled back. "Good Captain Biggles. Since, however, we are missing your GR-9 Jump Jet as the Turks have impounded it, we will be parachuting you near the Khoramabad base and you will perform the reconnaissance on foot."

It was quarter of an hour before the MPs had cornered Biggles attempting to commandeer a Vickers VC10 to fly to Istanbul, and instead bundled him and his parachute onto a Lockheed C-130 Hercules. It was a further two hours later before he was thrown into the black sky above Iran with a Stasi spy camera hidden inside his teddy bear. He would have parachuted earlier, but they had to release him from a death-like grip on the Hercules airframe as he screamed about frequent flyer miles to Istanbul.

In the empty gloom of the freezing air above Khoramabad, Biggles wondered about early retirement at the age of 110, but then cheered himself up when he realized he had his bear to talk to.

"You know Monty," he said to his habitual companion. "This reminds me of that time Matron took us to the London zoo on the Tube." At that moment, a tremendous barrage of flak opened up around him, as Iranian anti-aircraft gunners tried to shoot down the fleeing C-130

Hercules. "Although, I can't remember Matron being over Berlin with us."

With this, he fell asleep as the toll of three days without slumber finally caught up with him, all the while flak crumpled about him with all the danger of exploding sheep. In the morning he awoke wrapped in his parachute and surrounded by a dozen Iranian soldiers armed with their Khaybar assault rifles. They poked him with bayonets and sticks, and drowsily he grumbled about Sleepy Time in the kindergarten.

"Get Up!" said a solider with more facial scars than a cow at the wrong end of an abattoir.

"Whisky. Ice." Biggles mumbled as they dragged him to his feet and through him in the back of a Cobra armoured personnel carrier. "Have you cigars?" and then promptly fell back to sleep.

He awoke strapped to a chair and a bucket of water in his face.

"Heathens!" He ejaculated, then blinked and saw remarkably it was his latest arch-enemy Captain Arash of the Savama, or the Iranian secret police for those who missed the previous chapters.

"We meet again, Captain Biggles," he lit a cigarette and offered it to Biggles. "We have to stop meeting like this."

"Yes, let's have lunch at the Lyceum club, oh wait you're not a member."

"Really Biggles," Captain Arash pursed his lips in a smile.

"That's Captain Biggles to you," Biggles raised his eyebrows, "and I demand my rights according to the Geneva Convention."

"Remind me what those rights are?"

"You don't know?" Biggles blew a smoke ring, "Well first of all, any serving officer of the Royal Air Force is entitled to a free telephone call, tea and crumpet on silverware any time of night, holidays in Majorca during the off season, free dental care, and most importantly a date with Christine Keeler or Anna Chapman depending whom we're are at war with at the time."

"But Captain Biggles," the secret policeman sighed, "we're not at war, you are here spying on us, that makes you a spy and not a prisoner of war."

"Tosh - if you can fly a Camel, you can fly anything."

"That doesn't really follow from what I said, but you're still a spy."

"Prove it!" Biggles slammed the table with his fist. "I demand proof!"

Captain Arash pulled the head off Biggles teddy bear and removed the camera.

"Monty!" Biggles shrieked. "You murderer!"

"It's just a toy."

"And a serving officer in the Royal Air Force! That bear was the best autopilot I've ever known! This is a war crime!"

"We're still not at war, and it's still just a teddy bear."

"Prove it! Give me justice or give me liberty!"

Captain Arash pulled out the stuffing of the bear.

"Torture!"

"I always get the nutters," Captain Arash rolled his eyes.

They then attempted to torture Biggles with electric shocks and telephone books to the head, but every time they put a blindfold over his head he promptly fell asleep as three days without sleep in a Turkish brothel makes you immune to pain. Failing this, three hours later Biggles was put on a train to Turkey, and told not to spy on Iranian secret bases anymore. The bear they gave ten years hard labour for entering the country without a passport.

Biggles and the Weapons of Mass Destruction

"Biggles! Put down that cat!" Group Captain Wilkinson stormed into the officer's mess with a look that could curdle ennui.

"It may be a spy!" Biggles stared closely into the cat's eyes as it struggled to escape. "I caught it listening to me!"

"Put it down, I have a mission for you," Wilkinson threw a briefcase on the table and sat down with a thump.

"Can I take the cat? Could be a double agent?"

"No," snapped Wilkinson, "now sit down before I shoot you and the cat."

The cat flew out the window the instant it was let go. "There see!" Biggles pointed. "Escaping custody proves it is guilty."

"Shut up Biggles, this is important."

"So, am I - I'm the famous Biggles!"

"Which is why I'm risking you and not someone I might miss." Wilkinson slid a map across the desk and drew a circle around the Bushehr nuclear power plant in Iran on the Persian Gulf. "You are to be equipped with only a Yakovlev UT-2 monoplane and a Russian camera. We need you to fly over Iran and take photos and destroy the nuclear plant. Either way, the plant will be destroyed."

Biggles looked quizzically at the ceiling.

"Bother," he whistled, "but blow me down with a bunch of gorse berries, but how am I supposed to destroy a nuclear plant with just a camera."

"This is part of the plan, since the town of Bushehr has over 100,000 troops stationed around it, armed with scores of Russian ground to air missiles, state of the art phase array radar and a terrain so rugged camels commit ritual suicide rather than traverse it. You will almost certainly fail."

Biggles rolled his eyes and looked wistfully at the window the cat had left through.

"Still not following you, old strumpet."

"You are to be equipped with a Russian Lubitel 166 Universal single reflex camera. In advent of your certain capture or death, the spy mission will be blamed on the Russians and almost certainly start a small war between our good friends the Russians and our not so good enemies the Iranians. In the ensuing fog of war we are allowing our extremely good friends the Israelis to fly in and bomb the crap out the place and the world will be saved."

"Saved?"

"Saved by Biggles, I mean," smirked the Group Captain.

"I'll do it!" Biggles jumped up, "after all saving the world is what I do! Hang on, didn't I do this two chapters ago?"

"Yes, which is why the Iranians will not expect us to try the same plot twice!"

The Yakovlev UT-2 turned out to be an open two-seater, cockpit trainer left over from the Great Patriotic War, with all the handling characteristics of an Abyssinian goat in a wind storm. Biggles had tied the cat into the passenger seat and decided to call it 'Copilot Biggles' after himself; rationalizing if you are going to call a cat something - Biggles is as good a name as any.

"Pilot Biggles to Copilot Biggles, do you read copilot?" Biggles said into the mouthpiece once they had reached 10,000 feet.

"Meow!" the cat shrieked in terror as it struggled to free itself from the complex of webbing Biggles had used to tie it in.

"Meow it is, old bean," Biggles smoked a pipe and flew the airplane with his feet. He wasn't the famous Biggles for nothing. "What's our E.T.A.?"

"Meooow!"

"That soon, still time enough for a spot of tea, do you want Irish Breakfast or Earl Grey? I expect you'll want milk."

The cup of tea blew straight out of the cup and covered the moggy in Irish Breakfast. The sound of the aircraft, the rush of the wind, and the presence of captain James Bigglesworth was too much for it and Copilot Biggles relieved itself at every opportunity. The ground crew was going to have a fit when they saw the cockpit.

They soon flew into a sandstorm that not only filled the intake valves, it also covered the instruments and swamped the cockpit with sand up to the ankles. Under any other pilot, the plane would have gone down faster than an archdeacon on the under-fifteen rugby team, but Biggles managed to achieve the impossible by redirecting the exhaust pipe to the front of the intake and blew all the sand out - quicker than the above mentioned archdeacon discovering the Parents and Friends Association was due in the Gym in five minutes.

Meanwhile the cat had wriggled itself free and was climbing out on the wing, to get as far away as possible from the madman in the cockpit. Biggles was having none of this, put the plane on autopilot, an instrument the plane didn't possess and joined the cat on the wing for a spot of catch-the-frenzied-moggy, before finally dragging it back to the cockpit and tying it back in again. Just in time to stop the plane nose-diving into the side of a mountain.

Three minutes later the ack-ack over Bushehr opened up with all the fury of Madeline College all girls hockey team, as 100,000 Iranian troops let fire with enough ground to air missiles to bring down a category nine hurricane.

"I say Copilot Biggles!" Biggles whistled through his moustache, "the blighters are expecting us." As he ducked and weaved through the maelstrom of gyrating missiles with all the aplomb of Bradman discovering a dozen Bengal tigers hurtling down the pitch.

That Biggles was able to avoid be hit while flying a fifty year old plane, says as much about the inadequate training the Iranians gave their troops as it did about how amazing was the famous Biggles. It couldn't last long, and it didn't, as the plane suddenly gave up the ghost and pointed directly to the ground; a move the Iranian guards were not expecting as the plane came screaming towards them, accompanied by the caterwauling of both Biggles and his co-pilot. At the last moment, Biggles pulled a 90 degree turn out of the exhaust pipe and landed on the roof of the Bushehr Nuclear Power Plant.

It was the sort of move that only a Biggles could have achieved.

Instantly the anti-aircraft fire ceased as dozens of senior Iranian commanders stared anxiously at a plane perilously sitting right on top of the Iranian nuclear power plant. Biggles pulled the goggles onto his leather helmet and looked about to size up the situation. He was sitting on a giant concrete egg, the primary reactor of the power station and beneath him two megawatt thermonuclear reactors were slumbering. In every direction 100,000 Iranian soldiers were equipped with their Khaybar KH2002 assault rifles, or Saegheh 40 mm anti-personnel rockets, or most importantly Mersad Surface-to-air missiles and all were pointing them back at him. He also noticed that any move on his part meant the plane creaked ominously.

It was at this point the cat meowed.

"No Copilot Biggles!" Biggles yelled, "Now is not the time for kitty-litter!"

A bullhorn came sounding up the side of the dome.

"Who is that? Is this war?" the Iranian general yelled.

"I'm pilot Biggles and this is copilot Biggles."

"Wait - which Biggles is the Biggles?"

"Both Biggles is the Biggles!"

"There is only one Biggles!"

"That's me!" yelled Biggles getting irate.

"Then who is the other Biggles?"

"The copilot!"

A subdued whispering could be heard over the loudspeaker, until after some shoving and fierce punching, another general grabbed the handset. "Who is flying the plane?"

"I am! The famous Biggles!"

"And who's the copilot?"

"The not so famous Biggles, well not yet, but after today who knows."

"Is this an invasion?"

"Is this Iran?"

"Yes."

Biggles peeked over the side of the plane. "Then no not yet, but if you want to, you can surrender."

Again there was fierce muttering from behind the bullhorn, followed by a squawk as someone pushed the wrong button.

"We are holding you hostage, until the West surrenders."

"Righty-ho!"

Biggles stared furiously at the control avionics. "Fine pickle we're in here Co-pilot Biggles." He pursed his lips. "Speaking of food, time for a spot of tiffin. Do you have the marmalade?"

The cat continued rolling its eyes in fear and bit at the harness. Biggles searched around the cockpit for anything that resembled a tin of marmalade, then on reflection remembered he had no muffins to consume it with. He leaned over the side of the plane and yelled once more at his captors.

"I didn't bring the muffins, have you got any?" he whistled through his moustache.

Once more there was a jostling around the tannoy and each general fought for supremacy over the only functional bit of kit in the Iranian army.

"If you surrender, we have a lot for muffins down here, and cucumber sandwiches as well."

"Toasted or with crusts?" Biggles grinned.

"Both!"

"Ha! You'll need to get up early than that to fool the famous Biggles. Cucumber sandwiches are neither toasted nor crusted. Show me your muffins!"

This oddly translated into Iranian as an inexcusable insult and one of the generals would have ordered the Bofors 40mm anti-aircraft guns to open fire on Biggles on the nuclear reactor if the other generals had not wrestled him to the ground.

It was a classic Biggles Impossible Situation, the sort of unattainable adventure that only a Biggles could get himself into and then get himself out of without ending up in a box, and in this case there were two Biggles. The cat once more worked itself into a frenzy and escaped from its complex of webbing and dried cat vomit. Then it leaped out of the passengers seat and raced out to the wing where it hissed angrily and defecated over the side.

"That's it copilot Biggles," Biggles grinned, "you show them." Then he shrieked as the plane started tipping ever so slightly under the weight of the cat. "Stop showing them old bean! I can't trim the airspeed! Oh wait there is no airspeed!"

The ancient plane slowly inclined on top of the enormous dome, and everyone held their breath, until the cat –like all cats– ran up to the highest point around which was the other wing. Immediately the plane started tipping in the other direction.

All the Iranian commandos 'oohed' and 'aahed' as the plane see-sawed back and forth, they all started leaning from one side to the other matching the cadence of the craft.

The cat started slipping on the fabric of the plane and accordingly leapt onto the only thing with any purchase, which turned out to be the leather helmet on Biggles's head.

"Waaaaaaaah!" he screamed as needle sharp claws bit into his scalp. Biggles threw out his hands in sharp pain; one of them collided with the start button just as the plane started slipping down the side of dome.

"Waaaaaaaah!" screamed 100,000 Iranians as the screech of the air-frame dragged itself down the concrete like the world's largest nails on the world's largest blackboard.

The engine started just as the plane slipped off the side of the nuclear plant and it picked up just enough airspeed to avoid smacking to the ground like a dollop of strawberry jam.

"Gory! Gory! What a terrible way to die!" Biggles grinned manically he raced above the heads of the Iranian generals.

"Hit the deck!" came the sole voice of the leading general as the plane's propeller missed him by inches. Unfortunately, this was not only broadcast over the tannoy but also radioed to every platoon within a hundred miles, this had the overwhelming result that everyone was too busy spitting out sand to open fire, and Biggles had slipped across the Persian Gulf before anyone had the good sense to shoot him down.

Biggles was court martialed for failing the mission and the cat was awarded the King George Cross for gallantry in the face of overwhelming stupidity.

Biggles in Norway

Biggles landed on the Fjord and wondered if it was Wednesday, Holland or even reality. He hadn't seen Norway since the war so he didn't recognize it and more to the point he didn't even know what fjord is supposed to be; he also couldn't remember which war since there had been so many and it must be remembered Biggles had visited every war since the invention of flight. He looked around and wondered why Holland suddenly had so many reindeer, short cheerful laplanders in colourful dress and more importantly where were all the windmills.

His Harrier jump jet had been modified with pontoons to land on water this completely defeated the whole point of a Harrier-jet to land on the deck of small boat without the need for pontoons, but intelligence had never been a strong point with the Ministry of Defence. He had actually landed in Porsangerfjorden one of the most northerly fjords in Finnmark, 200 kilometres from the Russian border, and almost 2500 kilometres from his original destination. The actual flight plan had been a quick hop across the North Sea to land in Holland and demonstrate the new floating Harrier-jet to the Dutch as part of an arms deal in Amsterdam, but having had a rather enthusiastic late night of debauchery at the Wrens quarters in Portsmouth, he had fallen asleep two minutes into the flight and woken up with only five minutes of fuel left, inside the Arctic circle and suffering the sort of Bacchanalian hangover that would have floored Rabelais.

Biggles looked at a group of laplanders on the shore and wondered if they had any of those delicious Holland pastries Ginger kept rabbiting on about. What he wasn't to know that just behind him a Russian submarine armed with ten Verba surface-to-air missiles was pointed directly at him. The submarine had grounded during the night in the shallow waters of the fjord and was waiting for the tide to re-float; its conning tower poked out of the water like a very angry naval buoy. So as Biggles watched the laplanders and thought about breakfast, the captain of the stranded submarine glared at the aviator through binoculars and chewed his beard.

The commander had been on a secret mission to lay sonar detectors in the fjords as part of a Russian strategy to track the Royal Navy off the coast of Murmansk in preparation for the next herring war.

The probability of a plane from the RAF randomly landing not a hundred meters from his stranded ship never entered his ever suspicious Slavic mind. Remember the Russians belonged to a group of people whose country had been invaded so many times the translation of the Mongol's word for the Russian Motherland was now Sunny Holiday Camp; and the Russians still had a very vivid memory of the lavatories at the Siege of Sevastopol even if no one else had heard of them.

So if Captain James Bigglesworth curse of the Huns happens to appear out of the blue its a damn good chance an attack was imminent. The Russian captain had immediately ordered the surface-to-air missiles out on deck and prepared to die defending the glorious Motherland, even if technically he was in hostile waters and very definitely committing acts of espionage in a neutral country, but again bear in mind the astronomically high level of suspicious mind of the Slav. Biggles yawned and rattled around in the cockpit till he found his electric razor and removed the nights stubble, careful to avoid his magnificent moustache.

Captain Vasili Andropov stared in amazement at this act of bravado, it was the sort of stunt that won medals back home, although back home medals were still routinely awarded to milkmen who delivered on their monthly quotas. Vasili looked down at the missile launchers, scratched his beard, wondered what an electric razor felt like, for a flicker of a second he dared to hope.

Biggles blissfully waved to the laplanders herding ten thousand reindeer, and wondered if he could get a tow to the shore. Although he wasn't sure if reindeer could tow a ten ton ground attack jet but he was sure he was Biggles and for a Bigglesworth anything is possible. He pulled out a flare gun and shot off a round to get attention, this immediately stampeded ten thousand reindeer and the laplanders vanished with them.

"Bother, they could have at least offered me some pastries," muttered Biggles still under the impression he was in Holland. He looked around and to no end of surprise he found a complement of Russian sailors pointing rockets at him. "Hmm, must be the Dutch they live in barges don't they?"

Never one to let go an opportunity to impress the world with his innate cheerfulness he waved at them with the empty flare gun and looked about for a patisserie. Instantly Captain Vasili ordered his crew to open fire, only to discover to his horror that surface-to-air missiles simply don't work on surface-to-surface targets and the rockets flew over the hill and wiped out a large herd of reindeer that was conveniently nearby. At that moment the wind shifted on the fjord and Biggles' aircraft pivoted around to point his awesome array of GAU-12/U Equalizer Gatling gun and

Amraam missiles directly at the Russians who immediately surrendered and held their rockets above their heads. Biggles now convinced more than ever he had found the Dutch arms dealers waved back.

"Can you give me a tow?"

Several hours later in the captain's tiny cabin of the submarine Biggles found himself in the company of an inebriated Russian and a mangy dancing bear suffering from a painful case of phlebitis. Captain Vasili having discovered that Biggles didn't actually have the faintest idea he was in Norway and even less he was aboard a Russian submarine, was vastly enjoying himself; although the bear could not said to be enjoying himself at all. For several hours the Russian had been interrogating Biggles by plying him with him with vodka and stories from the gulag where he had grown up in Siberia.

"He name is Vladimir," grinned Vasili, "I named he after our glorious tyrant."

The bear sat in the corner cradling a bottle of vodka with an expression of eternal suffering, the room was so small he propped up Biggles like a bookend, as both Biggles and the bear stared at Vasili with amazement.

"Holland has a tyrant?" Biggles looked puzzled and scratched the bear behind the ears, "I thought you lot were an open free society. Pot shops, open street brothels and all that live and let live."

Vasili fell upon the floor laughing uproariously, he knew the English had a sense of humour but this was really too much.

"No, no, no," Vasili laughed at the ceiling, "you must stop, this against Geneva convention, we surrender. We defect to the west!"

"Defect?" Biggles, "from Holland? You and the bear?"

"Please, please stop!" Vasili rolled over and hammered the steel floor with his fist, "no more, stomach hurts, laugh too much!"

"So I take it - you do want to buy the Harrier?"

Vasili gave loose a squeal of what might have passed for laughter then doubled up in agony having burst an appendix from laughing too much and gave vent to a yelp of pain. He immediately went into shock and rolled about the flooring screaming in pain. The submarine sub-lieutenant ran in at the noise, followed by the ships cook, the doctor, and the fire control officer, as the room filled up with telnyashkas and obscene profanities in Russian as they attempted to get the Vasili onto the table. The cabin was so small that Biggles and the bear were crushed against the wall, charts and code books tumbled from bookcases, vodka bottles were smashed and Biggles was starting to wonder if the Dutch sense of a good time had gone too far.

At that point one of the sailors inadvertently stood on one of the bear's inflamed paws and it gave out a roar that deafened them all in the confined space. Instantly the cabin emptied including captain Vasili who suddenly realized appendicitis is less life threatening than an enraged drunken bear. Biggles not wishing to left out of the party followed closely behind pursuing the bear as this was the most entertainment he had had since accidentally crashing a Sopwith Camel into the Imperial Harem of the Ottoman sultan.

The entire crew raced up the conning tower and hung off the sides like rats deserting … no wait that simile is way too obvious, yelling at the captain that he should never have brought the bear on board in the first place, as he yelled back that he had inherited it in a game of Russian roulette and every Russian had a patriotic duty to own a dancing bear. The bear meanwhile was in a fury trashing the control room, ripping out cables and smashing monitors in a desperate search to find more vodka, as Biggles who well understood the necessity for alcohol in a the wardroom egged it on.

After a while a head popped down the ladder to the conning tower and ask Biggles if it was safe, this was met by a roar from the bear who after a month at sea had developed a worse case of claustrophobia than Freud had every encountered. The head disappeared followed quickly by the flight of the dancing bear and James Bigglesworth of the Royal Flying Corps found himself in charge of a Russian Delta class, and being James Bigglesworth of the Royal Flying Corps he used it tow the Harrier-jet into Amsterdam three weeks later and with no end of bravado tried unsuccessfully to convince the Royal Netherlands Air Force that this was the new attack vehicle everyone was raving about and would they trade it for a patisserie.

Bigglesleaks

Biggles was discovered sleeping in the back of the jeep cradling a bottle of Boodles Gin and nurse Hacketcrotch's underwear.

"Biggles I have a mission for you," Group Captain Wilkinson. "Let go that nurse."

Nurse Hacketcrotch leapt out the back of the jeep faster than an oiled salmon and Biggles moaned at the immorality of senior command.

"Sir - I was debriefing the corporal!"

"Stop that or I'll cut off your supply of Irish Whisky for a month!"

Biggles snapped to his feet and saluted. "Sir!"

"Really - that's all I have to do?" Group Captain Wilkinson raised his eyebrows hyperbolically, "wish I had known that years ago. Right then get to my office double time before I deport you to Somali."

Three hours later Biggles wandered into Wilkinson's office with a nurse on each arm wearing nothing more than an insolent grin.

"Damn," he sighed, "I thought this was the officers mess." The two nurses scampered as Wilkinson looked up from his desk and threw a copy of the King's Regulations at the door.

"Biggles! Sit down!" He pointed with a .455 Webley Mark I service revolver at the chair, and then pulled the trigger for effect. "Bang!" The back of the chair exploded and prompted Biggles to sit down with all the alacrity of a felled wildebeest.

"Sir!" Biggles would have saluted but he was smoking a Havana and didn't want to change hands, so he blew a smoke ring, which hung about Wilkinson's head for a full minute as Biggles' commanding officer glowered darkly.

"Biggles when I last saw you, you were at least half dressed, yet you are now wholly undressed." The Group Captain glared at our naked hero. "Care to explain why?"

"Nurse Hacketcrotch needed her clothes back. Sir!"

Group Captain Wilkinson rolled his eyes around the room in tired frustration. He looked idly at his Webley lying on the desk and wondered what a .455 Webley cartridge would do to Biggles head.

"Biggles I have a mission for you."

"Biggles will save the day, sir!"

"No, Biggles will do as he's ordered for once, and carry them out despite every opportunity to do otherwise. Biggles we have a leak on the base."

"So … a plumber?" Biggles waxed his moustache.

"Not hydraulic, you daft baboon, it's an information leak. Someone is leaking sensitive information to the Fourth Estate."

Biggles blinked repeatedly for a minute. "Is that anywhere near Epping?"

"No you blithering idiot, the Fourth Estate is the Press."

"I thought that was a Jeffrey Archer novel. Didn't he go to prison for it?" Biggles grinned impishly.

"One more remark like that Biggles and I'll demote you … again. Wait what rank are you now?"

Biggles' rank was in a constant state of motion as he successively saved the British Empire or was habitually court martialed for every offence known to the King's Regulations, from desertion in the face of the enemy to selling white slaves in Zanzibar – though in his defence it should be noted none of the slaves were actually British.

Biggles blew another smoke ring and thought slowly. "I think I may be Air Commodore this week or was it Air Marshal, not a hundred percent sure sir."

"So you outrank me?"

"Yes sir. At least for this week, but jolly who knows what those cocked hats up at the Air Ministry will come up with next week?"

"Right then," the group captain began slowly and poured them both a whisky, "As I mentioned before there is a suspected informant or spy on the base and I want you to go undercover and determine who they are and importantly whom the information is being sent to."

"So I'm to do this out of uniform." Biggles looked down. "Perfect disguise – what?"

Biggles spent the rest of the afternoon wandering around the airbase stark naked looking for anyone who looked like Jeffrey Archer or Peter Arnett. Surprisingly he ran in David Frost with a BBC film crew with a bewildered expression on his face and carrying a golf club.

"David," Biggles chewed worriedly on his cigar and wondered if he had met a ghost, "I thought you were dead?"

Biggles had known Frost during World War II when Frost was a cub reporter with the BBC delighting the American listeners as the sound of bombs fell on London during the Blitz.

"I was, or is it I am," Frost shrugged discouraged, "The National Health Service has a lot to answer for, let me tell you. What's even more confusing, is half my body was sold for medical experiments and I'm having to make do with rejects from the BBC props department. This leg was once part of a Doctor Who Cyberman and don't get me started about my pancreas."

"What are you doing here?" Biggles asked, smiling for the camera.

"I following up a story about information leaks from the air base."

"No you're not!" grinned Biggles and gave Frost a good thump on the shoulder which fell off, "that's what I'm doing."

"What have you discovered?" clicking the shoulder back in.

"Nothing."

"Is that why you're naked?"

"I'm undercover."

"You mean without a cover?"

"I am the Biggles." This was the sort of logic that had defeated Rommel during the North African Campaign when Biggles had gone naked for a whole month to ward off lumbago. "And what have you discovered?"

"The air marshal has been sending off twitters detailing troops movements along the Tigris."

Biggles paused and stared at the sky. "Don't suppose you know which air marshal?"

"There is more than one?"

"I'm rather hoping there is," Biggles sighed. "This twitter thing, don't suppose you know what that is?"

"Well, it's an email service that broadcasts snippets of information, complete nonsense if you ask me."

Biggles groaned and banged his head. "What does it look like?"

"Well you know, turn on a computer, connect to the internet and search for twitter."

"So it could in fact look like an ordinary computer screen, like the type when you fill in a signal intelligence report?"

"I expect so," Frost grinned seeing where this was leading, "but I've never seen one."

"Excuse me," Biggles did an about face, "I have to see a man about a dog."

By the time Biggles had made it back to Group Captain Wilkinson he had been demoted to mere captain again, not because he was guilty of disclosing sensitive information to the enemy, in fact it was sensitive information to the entire world, but because he was still stark naked and it just didn't do for an air marshal to go wandering about dressed like an

Eskimo in a bath house.

Biggles and the Ghost of Lawrence

Biggles came screaming out of the Sinai Desert so fast and so low, the sand spun up into columns of blinding dust that rose up two hundred meters and made Bedouin tribesmen cry out: "Al-Jinn! Al-Jinn! The Demon awakes!"

Which was a pretty good description of Biggles' mood that morning after his months furlough was cancelled for keeping an emperor penguin in the officer's mess refrigerator.

"Where the hell did you even get a emperor penguin?" yelled Group Captain Wilkinson on finding a giant penguin gorging itself on kippers and sardines in his refrigerator.

"Look old bean," retorted Biggles, "I'm pretty sure there is nothing in King's Regulations about keeping an emperor penguin."

"But keeping a pet is against Queen's Regulations," his superior officer screamed at the end of his tether. "It hasn't been King's Regulations since her coronation in 1952! Now get that bloody penguin out of here! You're grounded for a month!"

To be "grounded" has a completely anatropous meaning in the RAF compared to the rest of the world, notwithstanding the out-of-the-way notions of American sitcoms or even supposed schools of involving witchcraft and wizardry set in Scotland. In actuality, being grounded meant Biggles was required to do continuous airtime over the desert, this so annoyed him he was letting rip with the afterburner every time he saw another camel or an oasis. He had being doing so for the good part of an hour when his fuel abruptly ran out and he landed on a vast crescent dune just out of sight of the Suez canal. Bigglesworth jumped out of the cockpit and landed on the wing of his harrier-jet, without fuel he really was grounded.

The ochre sands shimmered to the horizon merging with a tangerine sky, buzzards and hawks circled beneath cumulonimbus clouds and the smell of acacia and tamarix flowers scented the air. To the north the crescent dunes of the Sinai swirled to merge seamlessly with the boiling chaos of the clouds. To the south, the superstructures of giant ships glided silently above an invisible Suez canal, passing through the desert like skyscrapers on a bizarre welsh caravan tour. A great angry desert storm filled with the promise of drowning floods, hailstorms and the cracks of lightening was headed his way. For anyone else this would have been a place of haunting beauty and threatening storm, but for the

Bigglesworth it was just bloody annoying as all he wanted was a whiskey and soda in one of the driest countries in the world.

Biggles fumed, as there obviously wasn't a ground crew running up to his jet to refuel, or even offer him a cup of Earl Grey and cucumber finger sandwiches. Biggles was obsessive about his cucumber sandwiches, he especially liked finger sandwiches made from white Pullman loaf, the slices so thin that sunlight peered through like Valenciennes lace, and the cucumber lightly sprinkled in salt and lemon juice, but as far as he could see there were no cucumber sandwiches - it was a cucumber sandwich desert. During the Anglo-Afghan war of 1919, Biggles had been bribed repeatedly by opposing drug-lords to bomb one-another compounds into rubble. For seventeen non-stop days he had survived entirely on cucumber sandwiches and opium, conveniently opium was the bribe so his motivation was extremely high and his accuracy extremely low, which meant that while he missed most of the war he succeeded in capturing the opium and cucumber market through the Khyber Pass.

The thunder of the storm began to bellow on the horizon, whirling dust dervishes spun across the dunes, and lizards burrowed themselves into the sands to escape the coming cataclysm. Biggles knew nothing about desert storms, if he had then he too would have been burrowing into the dunes, a desert storm is more like a terrestrial tidal wave, it smashes everything in its path, flattening man, beast and trees alike – you know there is a reason why there are no forests in the desert. Not that a bit of stormy weather was anything to faze the redoubtable Biggles, after all flying an open cockpit through a hurricane across the Sahara was a doddle for him, he hadn't been awarded the highest medal in the Egyptian military the grand cross of the Egyptian Order of the Nile for nothing, no he had won it in a game of whist with Winston Churchill.

Biggles maintained his fuming, after all he had nothing else to do, then he remembered the EPIRB, the Emergency Position Indicating Radio Beacon in the cockpit and switched it on. Not that he was happy about asking for help, but unless the 388 bus service from Wapping to Stratford took a major detour to the Holy Lands he was stuck there. The beacon began pinging with the regularity of a metronome with monomania, and he knew that in half an hour a friendly helicopter would be whirling above and it was back home in time for tea and cucumber sandwiches before the mess closed.

What Biggles didn't know was the name of the wind that was blowing at that moment from the Northwest – The Shamal.

The Shamal was the kind of wind that had no sense of humour at all about cucumber sandwiches, it was a very serious wind. It could blow non-stop up to two week days, screaming out of the Taurus mountains of Turkey, picking up dust and sand and hurling it skyward, then racing across the Negev and Sinai deserts intent on obliterating meteorological charts faster than they could be written. There the temperatures, even at lower elevations, soared above 120 Fahrenheit in the shade. In winter storms, it brought sudden heavy snows to the deserts, a layer of fine dust and snow choking and freezing anything or anyone that hadn't dug in.

The Sinai wasn't called the Devil's Carbuncle for nothing.

For Biggles this was unknowingly a bit of a disaster, as the ion charged sands effectively jammed all radio communications, he would have had better luck sending up a sending up a smoke signal by rubbing two camels together and hoping for a bolt of divine intervention. Scattered across the desert were more destroyed tanks left over from the Six Day War than the entire North African Campaign; and Biggles knew this because he had destroyed most of the tanks in both those campaigns. Rusty signs with minefield warnings clattered in the wind, the warnings were well justified by the bones of camels who obviously never learned to read. It was a forbidding terrible place and Biggles was now alone, as the lone and level sands stretched far away, then he noticed a bunker left over from the Six Day War and he wandered over to see if they had any sherbets.

The bunker was a modern Ozymandias, a monument to the folly of static warfare, bullet holes poked the concrete monolith that teetered on falling over as the sand ate away at its foundations and rust dissolved its iron. The ghosts of undecipherable signs in Arabic and Hebrew were faded by the sun, and goat droppings were everywhere.

Inside -to Biggles great surprise- he found something remarkably better than a sherbet, a Brough Superior 998 CC motorcycle under a tarpaulin in perfect condition. Left behind by a retreating film crew, it incredibly had survived the dry desert air and predations of the local goats, by virtue of being more British than the Royal Albert Hall on the Last Night of the Proms.

At that moment the storm fell upon the desert like a cataclysm, the sudden explosions of lightening bolts and thunder claps knocked Biggles to the ground. He screamed out in fear, reverting to the thing that terrified him most during his Edwardian school days: "Suffragettes!" remembering his nanny setting fire to mailboxes and chaining herself to policemen.

He leaped on the motorcycle and kick started it, it was British and had been built in Nottingham, so naturally it worked first time despite fifty years of sleeping like a mummy in the sands of the Pharaohs. Another detonation of thunderclaps convinced Biggles he was back on the Somme in 1916 with Fritz on one side and the Frogs on the other, he catapulted out the entrance into the wailing chaos of the storm, the wheels spinning in the sands and his scarf flying in the wind. The Shamal wind was like a the front end of a lorry going down the M1, it picked up Biggles and launched him downwind so rapidly he scudded across the crests of sand dunes one after the other. Anyone else would have been dashed to pieces, but just like the motorcycle Biggles was British.

A camp of Bedouin had pitched their blank tents to bulwark themselves against the storm. He tore through the camp at Spitfire speed, knocking out tent pegs and scattering camels like Kitchener's 21st lancer's charge at Battle of Omdurman. He left before he arrived, physically impossible but that's how the Bedouin described it to their descendants.

In a matter of minutes, the motorcycle covered a score of miles and neared the Suez canal, his speed was nearing 350 miles per hours, a Supermarine Spitfire with a supercharged engine would have had difficulty keeping up, unless it was flown by Biggles himself.

In a heart wrenching moment the Brough Superior 998 CC launched itself up the side of a steep embankment that left over from the Bar Lev Line of the Arab-Israeli War of Attrition, which sat beside the Suez canal dividing the Sinai from green fields of Egypt like biblical speedway ramp. Biggles flew 200 meters over a supertanker, bounced off a slow moving camel and landed in the first class section of the Cairo to Suez train. There to his amazement was an entire plate of cucumber sandwiches which he promptly helped himself to, before he was arrested for not having a passport, invading Egyptian airspace and stealing sandwiches.

Back across the Suez, the Bedouin had not seen anything this manic since Lawrence of Arabia strapped a Lewis automatic machine gun to the back of a camel and gone tête-à-tête with the Sultan's Turkish army. Forever after they called the event, - the Ghost of Lawrence.

Biggles and the Afrika Korps

On Thursday Biggles had been arrested for strafing the Pyramids in Egypt, his defence was the "bally things made such huge targets". On Saturday he was thought missing in action before he was discovered in a Alexandrian bathhouse in the company of a couple of houris, two empty crates of absinthe and a copy of Baudelaire's Les Paradis Artificiels, and then promptly arrested again. On Wednesday he was shot out of the sky by his own squadron after he attempted to shoot down a Luftwaffe Transall C-160 supply plane.

"What do you mean they're on our side?" Biggles was amazed, "they're the Boche, Jerry, Teutons, Krauts, Huns."

"The Luftwaffe is now part of Nato," Group Captain Wilkinson stared at the pistol on his desk and dreamed of using it. "What were you thinking?"

"But the very name Luftwaffe means the bad guys, old man," Biggles was perfectly inflexible when he needed to be. "Remember the Battle of Briton, the whole we few, we happy few, we band of brothers. We weren't shooting at pigeons over Trafalgar Square, no, we were shooting at Heinkels filled with people called Hermann, Hans and Fritz who were bombing the crap out of the pigeons in Trafalgar Square."

"That was seventy years ago!" the Group Captain's hand edged towards the pistol, "we haven't been at war with the Germans since 1945."

"Rubbish have you ever known me not to be at war with the Huns?"

It should be pointed out in Biggles defence, the two crates of absinthe had not only destroyed his long term memory, his short term memory, but also his declarative, procedural, episodic, semantic, retrospective and prospective memories. The only memory he had left was of Algy singing smatterings of Auld Lang Syne as he bailed out over Holland in a ball of flame during the Battle of Dieppe, so as far back as he could remember he really was still at war with Germany.

Biggles was in Egypt training their pilots as part of the lead up to Operation Desert Shield in Iraq, and had broken every mission statement and standing operating procedure there was. He would have been court martialed and broken to ground crew if it wasn't for the fact that Biggles had personally saved the British Empire over seventy-five times, since the 1916 Battle of Verdun when Biggles had shot the tail off Von Richthofen's plane, to the time he helped ensure an English a 6-3 victory over Germany in 1938 by appearing out of a cloud above the Berlin Olympic Stadium and strafing the German goalie.

When he found out the Luftwaffe was now part of Nato, serving in the middle east and about to transport Egyptian soldiers to the Persian Gulf for Operation Desert Shield, Biggles had reached for his Harrier-jet, flown sorties over German cruise liners in the Mediterranean and dared them to open fire. It flew in the face of all accepted reasoning and the historical evidence that Rule Britannia now ruled the skies with the help of the Luftwaffe. There hadn't been a more contrary inversion of reality since Bagpipes were deemed to violate the Geneva Convention after they had been used for enhanced interrogation techniques during WWII. Now to suddenly discover the Luftwaffe was flying into battle, albeit only to transport troops of a third nation, along side the Royal Flying Corps, had Biggles so angry he had repeatedly shot out the headlights of the German Ambassador's car in Alexandria to register a protest.

"Biggles," the Group Captain's fingers twitched on the handle of the pistol, "either you stop shooting at our allies or I will start shooting you myself, and that's final."

Biggles stormed off in a fury. He lay in his cot for a week dreaming up ways to turn the tide of battles so old that now moss literally covered them. Flies crawled over him in a war of contact and detachment, as he swatted them with the angry end of a .455 Webley Mark I service revolver blowing holes in the Nissan hut. After a week he devised a plan to capture Aqaba from German tourists then remembered Lawrence of Arabia had already done that, so he went back to swatting flies. Then he remembered he hadn't been drunk in a week and hit the bars in Old Cairo.

There were parts of Old Cairo that could have been right out of the boulevards of Paris, mansard roofs punctured by dormer windows sat above a streets with ancient books and the scents of pastries and sweets. The similarity disappeared with the cries and hacking spits of the Arab hawkers, as they chased tourists with cheap Filipino made Egyptian trinkets such as mickey mouse canopic jars, scooby-doo sphinxes, and cutest of all the banana in pyjamas mummies. The similarity with Parisian architecture completely died with the endless fast food stores selling American burgers and fried chicken, but Biggles was in a mood and he hungered for the Old Cairo during the occupation when he was a spy for the OSS.

He turned a corner and found himself face to face with a troop of German medical staff idling the morning away looking in shops, buying

American burgers and doing their best to ignore the hawkers. Biggles reached for his pistol then remembered he had used all the bullets aerating his Nissan hut.

"Blast!" Biggles chewed on his moustache and looked around for a bayonet, there was none to be had till he cast upon a hookah in a coffee shop.

"Please sir," the proprietor gestured to a seat, "coffee, tea, hookah, yes, yes."

"I have no time for this," Biggles glowered at the owner and rose up to his full six feet five.

"Please sir, small goats and monkeys if you prefer."

"What?" Biggles exploded, "that's outrageous, you cook monkeys?"

"Oh no sir," the owner waggled his head, his toothy grin expanding, "not cook, nice monkey, soft monkey."

"Swine," Biggles picked up the hookah and held it over the shopkeeper's head, "I am an Englishmen and an officer."

"I also have hashish," the owner grinned and winked.

"How much?"

Three days later Biggles was rereading Baudelaire's, Les Paradis Artificiels, having discovered the shop keeper included laudanum baklava in his menu, when the door broke down and a dozen MP's hauled him back to the squadron infirmary to have his stomach pumped out. He lasted there only a few hours before he remembered he was personally at war with the Luftwaffe, hijacked an ambulance and raced around Cairo trying to run over anyone with a suspiciously well tailored uniform. After eight hours of furious driving, destroying shop after shop and exterminating the chicken population of Old Cairo, when Biggles saw the Bundeswehr Medical Corps with their dark blue berets drove past him in another ambulance.

The squad of doctors were driving south to help with a local plague outbreak along the Nile, since the plague was now easily treatable with antibiotics it was considered a low risk opportunity for Nato soldiers to aid Egypt. Biggles was having none of this and took off in pursuit, gunning his ambulance to ram the back of the Bundeswehr ambulance.

"Teufelauto!" yelled the German driver and a chase began with Biggles chewing on his moustache and honking the horn to drive the dreaded Boche into the gutter. The Germans who had been nursed from childhood on the Autobahn to drive at insane speeds had a definite advantage over the increasingly erratic Englishman who drove through Garden City with its tranquil, tree-lined streets, hidden gardens, and ornamental palaces like a demon in a Coptic monastery. The two ambulances, sirens blaring, belted down the Nile Corniche past the U.S., British, and Italian Embassies on the left and the deep green of the Nile on the right, then suddenly the doctors hooked a right across the Monieb Bridge and headed to the Great Pyramids which shimmered distantly in the noon heat.

Biggles overshot the bridge, spun the ambulance twice before he regained control, catapulted across a five lanes of traffic, and landing in the flower bed of the Albanian consulate. Egyptian traffic, which at the best of times could be described at molasses dripping through a sieve, hadn't seen this much motion since the Pharaoh chased Moses to the Gulf of Suez and attempted the first underwater assault of the Sinai. This didn't prevent Biggles from restarting his engine, tearing across the bridge and scanning the horizon for his foe.

The Germans made it as far as the parking lot of the great pyramid of Giza before Biggles caught up with them. The chase broke out into open red-brown sands around the monument, a continuous obstacle course of tank-traps made from archaeological digs, American tourists badly riding camels, and Arab guides jumping out of the way. Every few meters the trucks bounced off rocky dunes and vaulted archaeologists hunkered down in pits, before careening off another sand dune and spewing sand over a years research into the Middle Kingdom. Finally the Germans broke an axle and jumped out of their truck as Biggles slammed into the other ambulance, shot out windscreen, ricocheted off the other truck to land on a camel. Thereupon he shook his head to clear himself and then started chasing the doctors around the ambulances, this went on for several minutes with Biggles becoming increasing dizzy till he fell off and landed head first in sand dune. The Doctors pinned Biggles to the ground and demanded to know what he was doing.

"Don't give me that, you rotters!" Biggles bawled, as they struggled to hold still his flailing limbs. "You shot Algy over Dieppe!"

"Dieppe? Dieppe?" the doctors shook their heads in disbelief, "who is this Algy?"

"What?!" Biggles was infuriated, "you don't even remember his name? You bastards!"

"We have never even been to Dieppe."

"Oh and I suppose you've never invaded Poland!"

"Me, personally, no," the doctor sighed and jabbed 50 cc of Valium into Biggles' neck. Biggles, however, after decades of experimenting with barbiturates had developed a powerful immunity to all analgesics, and continued to thrash about trying to remember where he had put his Webley service revolver. "Look, you have us mixed up with someone else! We are doctors, we're here to help."

At that moment the copy Baudelaire's Les Paradis Artificiels fell out of Biggles' pocket, and everyone looked at it. The doctors nodded their heads at each other.

"So you are a drug tourist? You like the hashish, hmm?"

"What?" Biggles looked askance, "Certainly not, I'm a serving British officer, we don't do that sort of thing. That's for research. You wont get more than name, rank and serial number from me."

"Yes, of course," the Doctor smiled and patted Biggles on the shoulder. After which they gave him to the Cairo traffic police and Biggles soon admitted to running red lights, attempted destruction of a historical site and impersonating a serving British officer. The last words of the German doctor as they pumped him with 200 cc of Sodium Pentothal and handed him over, were:

"You see, we still have ways of making you talk."

Spiderman

Saddam was hiding in a spider-hole, he knew this because there were spiders crawling all over him. He was on the run but he refused to admit his own people would give him up. Not he - the lion of the desert, the eagle of the sky, the guy with the gun on the balcony, and no one argues with a guy with a gun on a balcony if they know what's good for them. He would never be caught, he knew this because his astrologer had told him just before Saddam shot him, and that worried Saddam as the astrologer really should have seen that one coming. He was trapped between a rock and hard place, as in front of him the desert stretched far away, and behind him the city roared with attack helicopters and the world's most dangerous taxi drivers. It was hot in the sun, he wanted some water but he had run out of sewers to drink from, but at least the flies left him alone now the spiders had moved in.

Twice now he had tried to get food from the corner store, but they were out of his favourite, Turkish Delights, a good Turkish delight is hard to find if you're not in Turkey. This made sleeping all but impossible, and in his dreams he relived his years in power: "No prisoners! No prisoners!" he cried out in his sleep condemning thousands to death from hit squads in the night. Yet mostly it was reruns of Days of Our Lives that was really kept him up at night. For instance, how was Princess Gina Von Amberg really a trained art thief; and why on the day of her wedding to Bo did Gina try to shoot Marlena and Bo and Hope's son Shawn-Douglas – especially since Hope and Gina were the same person. To hell with the war he really needed his Days of Our Lives fix.

Saddam lay under a cardboard box hiding from his enemies in the Iraq government and the Americans. He was more worried about his loyal political opposition in Iraq than he was about the Americans, since the good thing about the Americans was how very democratic they were in their bombing. The Americans democratically bombed Iraq, they democratically bombed Libya, they democratically bombed the loyal opposition and they even democratically bombed themselves - with that sort of batting average all he had to do was hide out under this cardboard box till Christmas and there would be no left but himself.

He had been thinking of his hero Stalin during the Great Patriotic War and for the life of him he couldn't remember any incident of Stalin camping out in the desert under a cardboard box to hide from Hitler, but that problem of why Princess Gina Von Amberg were the same person kept coming back and interfering with his thinking, was Princess Gina Von Amberg even a real person?

It was at this point Saddam realized he was delirious with heat exhaustion.

Saddam crawled out from his pit and lay on the ground, a cool wind flowed over him like a fountain in Damascus. He watched the black and white plumage of Mesopotamian crows wheel above him and remembered seeing the same thing while travelling to Wadi Barada just west of Damascus in his youth. It had been spring and he thought it was the most beautiful place he had ever seen, the tall poplar trees were gold in the dawn and the river was an icy cold blue jewel that flowed along the railway to the mountains like a dream. Then he remembered it was in Syria that his cousin Sergio had touched him in all the wrong places so he put Damascus right out of his mind.

He stood up, he had had enough, he wanted a sherbet. After all, was he not Saddam Hussein Abd al-Majid al-Tikriti the lion of the desert, not Hussein the homeless vagrant. He was just east of the Tigris, palm trees and irrigation pipes were everywhere, he could smell the river barely 300 meters away. He stretched his limbs and shook his fist at the desert, then an helicopter flew overhead and he jumped back in this hole, his heavy eyebrows and haunted eyes peering out.

"No need to rush it," he thought.

After all, the Americans were crazy. Before the war they repeatedly said things like: "You need to cooperate, if you don't, we will hunt you down and we kill you." If he cooperated anymore he would soon be living in retirement in Albania. Saddam had been cooperating with the Americans as far back as he could remember. They said to him, attack the Iranians, so he attacked the Iranians. They said, don't attack the Iranians, so he stopped attacking the Iranians. They said pump more oil, so he pumped more oil. They said buy our missiles, so he bought their missiles. They said destroy your missiles, so he destroyed his missiles. If only they would make their minds up before all this cooperation killed him. He carried the white man's burden on his shoulders in the samples of anthrax, West Nile virus, smallpox and botulism sent to him from the American Centre for Disease Control. Ronald Reagan and George Bush Snr sent him VX nerve gas to kill the Kurds, they were true friends. Saddam had bought planes from France, ordered guns from Belgium, acquired missile launchers from Germany and drove tanks from Russia, all Europe contributed to the making of Saddam - and now they wanted to blow him up, it was so unfair.

Saddam stood up again and give the sky the finger, no American attack chopper could keep down for long. The Cradle of Civilization had seen the rise and fall of fiefdoms, kingdoms and empires, it was the centre of the world, the fertile crescent from which flowed all life. It all belonged to Saddam, the descendant of Hammurabi the lawgiver, Nebuchadnezzar the builder and Marduk the not so famous goat molester. He need fear nothing, he was Iraq and Iraq was him. He walked down to the river, and remembered that time in his youth he had made a daring swim across the Tigris River to escape being killed. Now was no different, he felt sure of it and nothing would stop his return to power. Then the helicopter came back and he dove in the water and hid in some reeds. These annoying pilots were getting in the way of his imagination.

Biggles was lost in a helicopter over Mesopotamia, the GPS had been shot out by ground fire, his compass was quite doolally and his bally sense of direction was permanently distorted following another mammoth battle with a crate of absinthe. Alcohol was banned in Arabia during the war for the Coalition, however, he reasoned that absinthe wasn't strictly alcohol so he drank it like lager till for four days without sleeping then stolen an Apache helicopter from the American airbase and flew around the desert blowing up anything that looked like a camel or a ziggurat. Biggles had never trained to fly an Apache, but Biggles had once escaped Colditz Castle flying an experimental German Wagtail Autogyro all the way from Saxony to Belfast so he could pretty well fly anything thing that had a tail rotor.

The sun had risen and Biggles was falling into micro-sleeps, this wasn't a problem for a pilot in the RAF who generally slept through most missions until the firing started, but he kept flying in circles and every couple of minutes a blazing sun would wake him up with a jolt and he would cry out:

"Hold me Erich! It's cold outside," as a result of a recurring dream about his greatest enemy the German ace Erich von Stalhein.

The wide sweep of the Tigris continuously revolved before him, side channels and oxbow lakes carved intricate filigrees across an immortal landscape of palm groves and wheat fields. This meant nothing to Biggles who had been in every War since 1914 and now had the world's second worst cast of Post Traumatic Stress Syndrome. He was known to throw grenades at his neighbours if they opened soda cans without warning him, he once jumped out of a commercial jet when they showed Shrek, during the 1966 FIFA World Cup he had repeatedly tried to fly a nuclear Polaris missile into Berlin when there was a risk the German's might win the game. The world had become a very strange place to him over the last century so the beauty of Mesopotamia meant nothing to him.

Biggles fell awake at the controls and in a moment of panic landed the helicopter without realizing he was still flying. The gunship landed right in front of Saddam who was equally surprised, for a second neither of them moved, then Biggles fell asleep again and Saddam started breathing again. It wasn't long before Saddam had dragged Biggles out of the Apache and tied him to a palm tree.

So began the interrogation.

Biggles had been tortured by the best, he had also been tortured by the worst he had after all played hockey against the under-fifteen girls team from Malton College. He knew pain, he knew ennui, he knew horror but nothing had prepared him for a conversation with Saddam Hussein Abd al-Majid al-Tikriti.

"Will Gina Von Amberg return in the next season?" Saddam stuck his beard in Biggles face and almost suffocated him with halitosis.

"Sorry what old chap?" Biggles coughed.

"Gina," Saddam wandered back and forth in delirium, "she is such a mystery to me, ever since I first saw her as Hope Brady when she was born in 1973 and then suddenly ten years later she is fully grown and married, and then ten years later she is found at Stefano DiMera's house with amnesia, so Stefano has the memories of the real Princess Gina Von Amberg, an accomplished art thief placing them on computer chip programmed Hope's head, so she becomes Princess Gina Von Amberg and why on the day of her wedding to Bo did Gina try to shoot Marlena and Bo and Hope's son? Why?"

Biggles looked around for a camera and Ashton Kutcher.

"Not quite following you, old bean, you're saying there was a wedding?"

"What I really what to know is are Hope and Gina the same person, and if so how did she shoot herself?"

"Really old chap," said Biggles genuinely puzzled, "I have no idea what you're talking about."

"Days of our Lives," the lion of the desert bit his bottom lip, "I've been out here for weeks and there is nothing else to think about."

"So with half the armies in the world chasing after you, your country in ruins, you're dressed in rags, lice and beards, and the thing you're worried about most is an American soap opera?"

"Doesn't everyone?!"

"Well yes, but they're not famous as you and me" Biggles grinned, "have you seen a doctor about this condition?"

"I saw Doctor Goldstein but then I had to shoot him because I told him too much."

"I see," Biggles started worrying again. What Saddam didn't tell Biggles was that Saddam had the world's worst case of Post Traumatic Stress Syndrome, even worse than Biggle's own condition, although Biggles was starting to suspect. Biggles dragged at the ropes and wished he hadn't swapped the combat knife for a flask of absinthe in his flight suit. "Absinthe!" he cried.

"What?" Saddam looked about in fear.

"Absent friends make the heart grow fonder."

"What are friends?"

"Here, look old boy, there is a hip flask in my pocket, how about we drink to old friends?"

Three hours later Biggles escaped on a barge headed down river and Saddam was captured in a spider-hole stoned out of his head on absinthe singing Auld Lang Syne.

"So you're telling me Gina wasn't really at the wedding, it was the real Gina, no you mean it was the real Hope?" Saddam later asked the hangman.

Biggles and the Art of Angling

Biggles was off the coast of Kuwait looking for somewhere to fish, he had heard there were sailfish of prodigious size in the waters and was wondering if he could use his Harrier-jet as a fishing boat. He had read Izaak Walton's 'The Compleat Angler' and now had complete confidence it would work. He flew an open cockpit Harrier-jet, and this took him back to the good times over Flanders in his Sopwith Camel battling the Hun, waving at the farmers daughters and drinking champagne. Flying open cockpit made as much sense in a Harrier-jet as sticking a brick on a bumblebee and expecting it to fly, but it was the only way he could get the rod out the window. It was only possible to fly an open cockpit Harrier-jet by its extraordinary ability to hover just above the ground, which Biggles was now doing, as he skated across the sea sending up a plume of water that could be seen for miles. This had the added advantage that he didn't headbutt the canopy every time he ejected, which on last count had happened at least on every flight for the last two months and he would have run out of jets long ago if he hadn't kept stealing them from the Americans.

Biggles out of the corner of his eye saw a low another plume of water far off to Iran moving parallel to his plane. Biggles eyes were keener than a hawks, he could spot a dragon-fly half a kilometre away, and this was the key to his amazing piloting skills, his ability to spot the enemy long before they even knew he was there. Unfortunately before taking off that morning Biggles had downed a bottle Irish Whisky to keep him warm in the dawn's freezing cold, so now his eyes jiggled about like bumblebees on amphetamines.

He tossed the fishing rod and closed the canopy.

"To hell with fishing," he thought. "That's what Harrods is for."

Slowly banking left he pushed on the afterburner before roaring across the Arabian Gulf in a tornado of whirling foam and spray. Diving up and down across the water in perfect unison the waves it was if he was glued twenty feet from the water by an invisible ruler. The instruments showed he was nearing the border of Iran, he slewed to the left and kept pace with the unknown craft moving West. Small medieval forts left over from the middle ages floated past on the shore, their square crenelations contradictory not just with the land but the age itself. Through the haze that swirled across the sea a shape appeared, it was a military hovercraft equipped with SAM missiles and miniguns, as fierce any Kraken that had ever swam the Mediterranean sea.

"I've wonder if it's a Channel Ferry?" Biggles said, whose eyesight that morning could at best be said to be blind drunk.

Surprisingly, and it is surprising, Iran once had the world's largest hovercraft fleet and had now built the world's largest hovercraft, and even more surprising most of this beast was made in Birmingham in secret with the code word Ifrit. The Iranians were able to achieve this by telling the British engineers they were a ferry service from Normandy. How MI5 never picked up on it, was even more startling than the possibility that Birmingham still had an engineering industry. It was so secret the Admiralty didn't know they had built it till it sailed past the Royal Regatta and accidentally rammed Her Majesty's Yacht Britannia. The Iranian captain fled in a bank of fog into the Bay of Biscay, and a diplomatic disaster was avoided by blaming drunken fishermen from Brittany refusing to sail on the right side of the ocean and putting it all down to French manners.

What put the Ifrit in a class of its own, was firstly its enormous size of over 200 feet in length and secondly a carrying capacity of five hundred long tons. This was four times larger than anything the Russians had, putting their Zubr class military hovercraft well in the shade. For while the Zubr could only carry three main battle tanks the Ifrit could carry an astonishing eight tanks, it carried over two thousand troops and had its own helipad. But on top of that it had stealth technology and its ducted fans were virtually silent. This wasn't a ship, it was a fortress upon the sea.

British technology at its best had, of course, being given away to the wrong people. This had happened so many times over the Empire's history that the rest of the world didn't look upon Britain as a closed book military technology more like the local library with no penalties on later returns. English engineering had given the Japanese their first aircraft carrier and torpedo bombers which were soon used to sink HMS Prince of Wales and the battlecruiser HMS Repulse during the Battle of Singapore. Sir Stafford Cripps had during the Cold War simply given the Soviets complete drawing, specifications and working models of a Rolls-Royce turbojet engine as a gesture of international diplomacy and overnight comrade Stalin had one of the best fighter aircraft of all time which proceeded to shoot down more British pilots in the Korean War than anything else the communists had in their arsenal. Napoleon, voracious reader that he was, had first learned the importance of field artillery from a book on naval guns by a certain Horatio Nelson and that mess wasn't cleared up until Waterloo.

Part of Biggles' brain was suggesting it was time he flew back for crumpets and gin, another part just wanted to know what in Poseidon's net was trawling up the coast. He went closer, waggling his wings barely a hundred meters from the monster, and not surprisingly the captain of the hovercraft ordered General Quarters and targeted Biggles with enough fire power to crack the sky. This amused Biggles who had been shot at so many times he had now regarded ack-ack as the warm up before the rugby game. He flipped the Harrier-jet over and landed on the helipad so fast that no one had the chance to order open fire. Biggles got out and went for a saunter around the deck, admiring the enormity of it all.

It never occurred to him that this wasn't the Channel Hovercraft.

It was well made, as are all things made in Birmingham, but the Iranian flags seemed out of place with the deck quoits, swimming pool and badminton nets. It must be pointed out the lads in Birmingham really did think they were building a Mediterranean cruise hovercraft for the French, although at some point they should have wondered about the General Dynamics Phalanx close-in weapon system Gatling guns that fired armour piercing tungsten or depleted uranium rounds were doing on the blueprints - but Bank holiday was coming up so they rushed through the final build.

It took ten minutes before the crew cornered Biggles who had discovered the sauna on the aft deck and was looking for a gin and tonic. "Massage please," said Biggles as he stretched out on the table of the sauna amazed that the cross channel ferry now had massage rooms.

It was simply too outrageous that the crew and captain froze, wondering what to do, obviously Biggles wasn't a spy. No matter how many reruns of 007 in Casino Royale they had watched, they knew no one did this in reality. No, this had to be part of something sanctioned by the Iranian high council and they simply didn't get the message. The Admiral, who had no idea what the rank on RAF flight suit laying on the chair was supposed to be, was very worried he was addressing a superior officer,

"Massage!" the Admiral ordered his Captain.

"Massage!" the Captain ordered a Lieutenant.

"Massage!" the Lieutenant ordered an Ensign.

"Steady on, chaps, just one," Biggles held up his glass and shook it, "and fill the glass dying of thirst here. Bottoms up!"

This really confused the Admiral so he turned around, leaned over and stuck his behind in the air, this was followed in short order by the Captain, the Lieutenant and Ensign bending over the presenting their posteriors to Biggles, it was after all the Navy.

Biggles on finding his glass wasn't being filled and the room was now filled with white bell-bottoms jumped off the couch and went in search of a bar. What Biggles didn't know was that Iranian special forces were also on the ship and they were unlikely to bend over. Biggles was still stark naked when he walked past them with his flight suit over his shoulder. They too were fooled by the absence of threat in our hero and choose to look the other way as in their culture nakedness it is extremely embarrassing, as he walked away they did manage to surround his Harrier-jet and demand its surrender.

Next Biggles made his way to the bridge ordered the pilot on pain of death to head for the nearest harbour with nude bathing and a bar, then headed back downstairs in search of the galley hoping to find some drinking sherry. Biggles didn't know how World War III would be fought, but he knew World War IV would be fought with brothels and bars like all the wars before.

By this point the crew was starting to wake to the fact that Biggles was in no way a part of the Iranian Navy and was quite possibly a Somali pirate, admittedly a Somali pirate with a profuse amount of ginger hair and a Harrier-jet, but nevertheless they had a shrewd idea he never attended the Iranian Naval Academy at Bandar-e Abbas with them. An alarm was broadcast across the ship to hunt down the pirate and preferably shoot on sight.

Biggles, however, had gotten lost again and ended up the auxiliary control room of the Phalanx Gatling guns.

How the Americans had allowed the Iranian navy to be supplied with them was a question of logistics that MI5 would rather not answer, in much the same way they always managed to avoid answering the question 'how the hell' were Donald Maclean, Guy Burgess, Anthony Blunt and the other members of the Cambridge Five able to supply the KGB with sensitive information for so long it became a running joke in the Kremlin.

Biggles was looking for a light switch in what he thought was the galley, when he accidentally fired the Gatling guns which then proceeded to demolish most of the forward deck of the hovercraft, including the lifeboats and the bridge where the officers had regrouped to mount the search. Within seconds most of the superstructure vanished under the impact of 6,000 rounds per minute of armour piercing high explosive incendiary that essentially vaporized the decks. Surprising no one was hurt this was probably due to the Iranians setting the fire control system to mute. Biggles satisfied the ship was out of booze, wandered back to his Harrier-jet, took off and flew back to Kuwait before the ship sank. It was only the next day when filling out his logbook that Biggles remembered he wasn't in France.

Operative

Biggles found himself in a run down cafe in Athens, smoking Russian cigars, drinking Greek coffee and trying to divine what his mission was meant to have been. He had been there several hours and still had failed to come up with a convincing explanation for his waking up that morning in a Greek prison, clutching a very sweaty fat Greek man who kept muttering: "Ave maria," over and over into Biggles' ear, before the prison guards kicked him out and told him to find a hotel that catered to his particular brand of weirdness. The back of the cafe was so dreary and the coffee so atrocious that even Zorba the Greek would have left, but Biggles remained there in the vain hope the waiter would stop belly dancing.

It occurred to him he had been so drunk the night before that he had suffered short term memory loss, this he refused to believe as he could never remember having had this before. It also worried him he might have post-traumatic amnesia from repeatedly crashing planes; or the repressed memories of his childhood as a cabin boy on the Titanic had finally bubbled up; or what he feared perhaps the most - posthypnotic amnesia of being hypnotized by gypsy slave traders.

This, however, didn't explain how he had travelled a thousand miles from the Forward Operating Base in Iraq to the middle of what he could only presume was somewhere north of London. Despite the fact he was surrounded by Greek waiters, Greek coffee and had woken up in a Greek prison, Biggles still wasn't sure what country was in, but he did know he was Biggles - so something, no matter how inexplicable, was bound to turn up. The only clue he had a brown leather valise briefcase handcuffed to his wrist and lacking a key. He had tried picking the lock with a bobby pin, he had tried shooting off the lock, and most ingeniously he had tried lying down beside a tramline and hoping the tram would run it over and break the lock, but this only resulted in a dozen trams being stopped around Athens and his being cited for being a public menace.

Now late in the afternoon, over cigars and a latte so appalling bad he thought it was mud, he pondered if he had finally gone mad. When a stranger appeared and sat in front of him wearing a newspaper. This is not to say the stranger was holding a newspaper, no, he was in fact wearing a newspaper and holding his clothes. Biggles watched and wondered if this was one of the circumstances best handled by looking the other way, or pulling out his .455 Webley Mark I service revolver and demanding he be left in peace.

"Biggles."

"I'd say yes, but I'm afraid of you."

"You will have to forgive me for my appearance, but after the escape last night in the sewage systems I really needed a wash." The stranger grinned. "This city needs to flush more often."

Biggles looked around the cafe and saw no one was paying them any attention. So he surmised it was perfectly normal at three o'clock in the afternoon for this man to be dressed in nothing more than a copy of the Balkan Chronicle. The idea that this was how all the locals conducted interviews also occurred to him, so Biggles ordered two more Greek coffees and settled back to be entertained.

"Excellent you still have the briefcase," said the stranger, "I was worried you may might have lost it during the escape. I still have the key, we must deliver the plans to the consulate by no later than 11 pm tonight."

Biggles watched and chewed on his Russian cigar, he knew something was happening, and he knew he was involved, but most importantly he knew he was flat broke and he knew someone had better pay for all the coffees he had bought or it was back to washing dishes. The man had a solitary blue eye that was covered with a blue mist, accompanied with a scar that ran from his brow to his lip, it was the sort of thing that in the 19th century Prussian generals paid a small fortune in dental fees to acquire. He was also dressed in a sort of Scottish gamekeeper-tweed that made a lot of sense when stalking deer in the highlands but was a portable sauna when worn in torrid Athens. Biggles decided he was going to play this calmly until either his memory came back or he found a reason to shoot the stranger.

"Yes," Biggles said slowly. "So about the escape?"

"From the Turkish embassy." The stranger shrugged. "Yes, dashed tricky business that, you would think they would give us more of a background briefing on these missions."

"Turkish embassy," Biggles lolled his head back on his chair as if ruminating about a Pythagorean principle and still hoping to winkle something out of the stranger. "Missions."

"I say Biggles are you alright?"

"Biggles." Biggles attempted then corrected himself. "Bigglesworth is my full name. So pleased to meet you."

"Sorry old man, Reginald Grenville-Mackenzie, Foreign Office attaché. Call me Reggie. I thought we had been introduced."

"Jetlag," Biggles had discovered that whenever he had lost or forgotten something vital all, he had to do was mention jetlag and instantly people were forgiving. "I don't suppose you could remind me what we were doing last night?"

"You forgot what the mission was last night?"

"Well I do have a hectic schedule and you have no idea how much jetlag a jet pilot gets over his lifetime. It's all to do with the sun always rising in the East."

"I never thought of it that way," Grenville-Mackenzie look bemused. "After we we met at the gypsy camp..."

"A-ha!" Biggles sat bolt upright and pointed a finger at the ceiling. "Hypnotized by gypsy slave traders! That's why I can't remember."

"You can't remember a thing?"

"I remember I'm the famous Biggles, what more do I need to know?"

"Quite." Reggie raised an eyebrow. "Well you need to know is that you are carrying the Turkish plans for the invasion of Balkans in your briefcase for a starters."

"The Balkans," Biggles let this idea roll around in his head, "isn't that in Yorkshire?"

"Er no, we're here in the Balkans right now, this is the Balkans." Grenville-Mackenzie arched an eyebrow at his accomplice. "The Balkan Peninsula is basically all of south-east Europe including Albania, Bulgaria, Croatia and Greece."

"Greece!" Biggles again stood bolt upright and pointed a finger at the ceiling. "That would explain why I keep seeing the Acropolis up there! On that hill thingy."

"The Acropolis is the hill thingy." Reggie looked somewhat worried. "You thinking of the Parthenon."

"The temple thingy on top of the hill thingy?"

"Yes in the middle of the other Greek thingys."

"And come to think of it - that would explain all the Greek waiters I keep meeting. Mind you, Yorkshire was close."

"Um."

"Not close?"

"Not quite."

"Devon?"

"No."

"I say old man," Biggles was aghast, "we're not in Belgium are we? Last time I was here there was hell to pay. Something to do with the Kaiser and France I seem to remember, yes it's all coming back now. I say it's awfully fun being Biggles and all that."

"No, we are in fact in Greece, and you are in fact acting as a courier for the RAF."

"Just a courier?" Biggles looked downcast. "Oh bother, suddenly being Biggles is not quite so much fun."

"People are trying to kill us."

"Hurrah! Biggles to the rescue!" stood bolt upright once more and punctured the ceiling with his hand. "Waah! Oh dear, have you got a band-aid? I may have cut an artery."

Biggles and Grenville-Mackenzie left the infirmary after Biggles repeatedly tried to ask the girl behind the counter if she wanted to fly in a jet, and he repeatedly tried to stuff prescription painkillers into his pocket. They only lost the police by the time they had fallen in with a group of Canadian tourists who thought he was a tour guide with a background in classical history.

"And this is the Arc de Triomphe," Biggles pointed out a men's outdoor lavatory.

"I thought that was in Paris?" countered one of the tourists.

"It's on loan from the Tate Gallery," Biggles shot back. "And that large structure over there is a work by Kandinsky."

"It's a bus stop."

"It looks like a bus stop, it tastes like a bus stop but really it's abstract art."

This was met with several: "Oohs" and "Ahs" accompanied with the obligatory photo with Biggles as the centrepiece.

"And here for the pièce de résistance," said Biggles dragging up one of the few French words he remembered from his time in the French underground and pointing at a small news stand, "is the Hôtel Ritz."

The news stand was opposite the Arch of Hadrian and could not have been less Hôtel Ritz. A tired Greek news seller looked back at the party, then looked over the counter at the sign in front of him and then back at the tourist group in bafflement.

"Biggles we need to get moving," Grenville-Mackenzie pulled at Biggles' elbow and tried to drag him away.

"Biggles?" one of the Canadians said in surprise, "are you any a relation of the famous Bigglesworth?"

"What do you mean relation of the famous Bigglesworth? I am the famous Bigglesworth."

"Shouldn't you be dead?"

"The Empire needed me and no Hun bullet could kill me," Biggles stood up on the news stand, "believe me I've tried, I've been shot so many times my internal organs have completely dissociated from me and are now living an independent existence in my lower abdomen."

"No I mean, shouldn't you be dead because you must be over one hundred and ten years old."

"You know no one has ever mentioned that before, that may explain why I keep getting telegrams from the Queen, I just thought she was still keen on me. - Ah, Queen Victoria the times we had in the south of France."

"There he is!" a whistle blew and a dozen Hellenic police raced up the hill.

"Run Reggie Run!" Biggles screamed, "it's the Fuzz!"

Biggles and Grenville-Mackenzie disappeared like a mist before an Odyssean rosy-fingered dawn, and vanished in a backstreet as Biggles demonstrated a hitherto unknown ability to lift a drain cover and dive into three thousand years of Athenian sewage.

"Bother!" Biggles spat out something that had decided to take a evolutionary path that even the Royal Society could not have predicted. "Now I remember - This is Athens!"

Three hours later they had successfully spelunked their way across half of the city and arrived under the British consulate. They found their way was blocked by a large Turkish colonel, who holding a torch and a broom-handle Mauser. The colonel was pointing the end of a pistol that had caused more fatalities than Turkish traffic after a particularly hard day at the bazaar.

"The papers," the colonel informed them.

"Papers? What papers?" defended Biggles.

"The ones in my briefcase?" the colonel pointed at Biggles' offending arm.

"This briefcase?"

"That briefcase."

"I don't have a key."

"I do have a gun."

"He has the key!" Biggles pointed enthusiastically at Grenville-

Mackenzie

"Traitor!" yelled Grenville-Mackenzie enthusiastically in response.

"Look if you're willing," Biggles having had enough for one day explained to Grenville-Mackenzie,, "we'll put the briefcase on you, I'll take the key and he can shoot you, but until such time, you give him the key and I'll go get a Scotch and soda."

After some grumbling on the part of Grenville-Mackenzie about honour, traitors and how Eton still had a better Rugby team, the key was handed over and the briefcase was unlocked.

"What's this?" The colonel said, and all three looked where the torch was shining inside the valise. "Where are the papers?"

"Oh those papers," Biggles shrugged. "They're still back at the cafe, I finally picked the lock on the briefcase and ditched them. Jolly well took me half the day to get the bally thing off. Can't tell you how glad I was to see the end of them."

But the discussion was already over as the Colonel and Grenville-Mackenzie had run off down the sewer. "Well you could have left me a candle at least! You bastards!" Biggles yelled after them, then looked fearfully around the dark tunnel. The smell of methane, three year old Moussaka and anchovies all but overwhelmed his sense of smell, but generations of destroying his palate with cigars, cheap whiskey and the occasional WAAF had made him immune to the odour.

Then Biggles heard a noise in the dark, a soft indistinct noise that crept along the spine and settled in the base of the skull like a needle.

"Hello? Algy? Is this the Christmas party?"

Again the noise echoed about the chamber, making the hairs not only stand up on his neck, it made his moustache stand out like the wings on a Sopwith hammering down upon the Hun.

He whispered in a hoarse voice: "Now is the winter of our discontent, made glorious summer by this sun of Devon."

This time the noise was closer and undeniably closer, Biggles put out his hands to ward off the incomprehensible and found a wall that dissolved into mist.

"Jeremy ...I know you're there!"

Again the sound of the unknown surrounded by silence .

"Jeremy I swear it wasn't me!" Biggles began to sweat profusely, "I wasn't there!"

The silence grew closer. This noise wasn't in the flight manual for a DC-10 Douglas, this was more palpable than the senses would allow, a sound that hollowed the soul and left the hearer wondering if the sound was coming or going.

"Away, Jeremy away!" Biggles hissed at his silent shadow, "Away."

The silenced hissed back at him, edging along his shoulder and onto his neck.

Biggles grew frantic and battered the invisible air to keep it away.

"It's true! I'm sorry!" Biggles screamed, "I never should have left you in the desert! But it was the long weekend and the bars were opening early! Jeremy for the love of god forgive me!"

The silence crept into his ears and hissed like an ocean captured in a shell. Finally Biggles broke and he pulled out his Webley pistol and began firing off randomly, the echoing explosions deafened him but instead of driving the sound away it only made it made it worse.

"Jeremy I'd didn't mean to kill you - you bastard!"

Then Biggles fainted. The next day he awoke in the Athens hospital surrounded by the British consul and the head doctor.

"Commander Biggles, you're lucky to be alive. "

"I'm the famous Biggles, I'm lucky at everything."

"Well at least you know who you are," the consul smiled and patted him on the arm, "the doctor here says exposure to a methane gassing often causes memory loss and auditory hallucinations. If you hadn't fired off your pistol those gypsy children never would have found you in the sewers."

"I knew it!" Biggles sat bolt upright, "Gypsies stole my brain."

School Days

It was looking to be a good week, for it was Tuesday and Biggles had succeeded in not crashing more than three planes. The ground crews were running a sweepstake to see how many he would wreck by years-end. At present the score was up to fifty seven write-offs, twelve were salvageable, and one he landed on the mess they couldn't get down without a crane. His speciality was pancaking them into the tarmac while yodelling in the Swiss dialect of Apfelschnaps.

"I say Biggles," said ground-crew sergeant Witherby, "smashing good smash," as they helped Biggles out of the wrecked canopy of the Douglas DC-3 he had stolen from the Scandinavian Airlines. "Group Captain Wilkinson wishes to see you sir."

"Is it a happy Group Captain Wilkinson or an unhappy Group Captain Wilkinson who wants to see me?" Biggles pulled back his goggles and blinked.

"A happy Group Captain Wilkinson," Witherby saluted.

"Excellent."

In the back of the airplane were a couple of Norwegian airline hostesses who still thought they were in Finland. "What shall we do with them sir?" asked Witherby.

Biggles stroked a moustache that had seen more action than the Light Brigade at a Sevastopol brothel.

"Post them to my barracks and delivery three crates of Veuve Clicquot 64' to my room."

Group Captain Wilkinson was not happy, indeed Group Captain Wilkinson was close to being irritated, this irritation vanished however, as Biggles walked in and dropped a kilo of Istanbul hemp and on his desk.

"Mission accomplished sir!" said Biggles as he jumped in a chair.

"What mission? I thought you were on leave?" Wilkinson looked with pleasure on the bundle. Biggles had discovered his commander was a raging drug addict and had bribed him with everything from Scopolamine, Albanian opium, red phosphorous and most perilously injecting distilled Stilton Cheese.

"I was sir, but an opportunity arose that made it all but impossible to ignore."

"Which was?"

"I rescued the Sultan's wives from his harem."

"You mean the Grand Vizier wives from his harem, as in the

Grand Vizier of the Ottoman Empire?"

"Yes sir, and jolly good sport it was too."

"Biggles no, bad Biggles. You've gone too far this time." Group Captain Wilkinson opened the package of hash on his desk and hurriedly stuffed some in his pipe. "There is no Grand Vizier of the Ottoman Empire, it's now the President of Turkey, they went democratic in 1920. But I do have message from the President requesting his daughters be released from the madman who kidnapped them from their school yesterday."

"School?"

"School."

"Ah."

"Ah indeed young Biggles. Where are they now?"

"I flew them to Constantinople, sir."

"You mean Istanbul?"

"Pretty sure it was Constantinople, sir"

"No I think they changed its name in the Fifteenth Century. Really Biggles you must catch up with the times."

"It's not me sir, I had a classical education in Malton Hall School, between the beatings, the booze and the buggery I never had time for Geography."

"And yet you managed to become the world's leading aviator."

"Gosh yes sir."

"So technically you didn't kidnap them at all, you just took them on a joy ride around Istanbul and then managed to leave the daughters of one of our key allies in the middle of Turkey."

"Yes sir, after all I am Biggles."

"Biggles it amazes me how you ever made it this far."

"That's what my Geography teacher used to say between all the beatings, the booze and the buggery."

Group Captain Wilkinson looked long and hard at his top Ace, this was mainly to do with pipe-full of hash he was inhaling, but he was also thinking how to punish Biggles' latest infraction..

"Biggles," he said thoughtfully.

"I say gosh that's me," grinned Biggles who had been as high as a kite since the President's palace in Istanbul.

"It's time you went back to school and did some proper training."

Biggles fell off his chair and went into the fetal position.

"Please sir," he pleaded gagging, "anything but school."

"It's for your own good."

"Rabies give me rabies, the bubonic plague, anything but ninth form! The horror! The horror!"

It was no use, the Group Captain had made up his mind, not to mention he was running out of airplanes for Biggles to crash, and within the week Biggles was shipped off to school with a bag of hash, a lifetime supply of prophylactics and two bemused Norwegian airline hostesses.

The school was strange, stranger than the mental institute it had been built upon, this nightmare of the seventeenth century masquerading as a college, was a cross between the tomb of the damned and a Van Diemen's Land outhouse. Towers and ramparts soared up above the countryside and fell back down indifferent to local building permits and any plan the architect might have dreamed. Cows and herdsmen scurried past, spitting over their shoulders to ward off an evil which they could never identify and would not shake until the sun rose the next day. Crows would land for a moment then inexplicably explode in a burst of fire. In the year of our lord 1648, Oliver Cromwell and his New Model Army had thundered across England into Hertbury with 10,000 god fearing and hell damming Puritans right up to this school, then upon taking one look at this establishment of learning had continued thundering right past, vowing never to return -There was something truly malevolent about it.

Biggles felt right at home.

"No Matron! No!" he screamed to no avail as he was assigned digs in the left wing of the college, the one overlooking the sewage pit and the witches ducking pole. "I'm a captain in the RAF!"

"Yes deary, and when you learn how to behave you can go back to the RAF but for now you've got a semester of Latin, Mathematics, English and Geography to get through."

"No! Not Geography!" He screamed, but Matron was having none of his tantrums, since after fifty years of raising boys into men she knew how to beat the crap out of them and feed them pudding without complaint. In his earlier time at Malton Hall School Biggles had managed to escape seventy five times before he graduated, as a school dux with certificate in wood-craft and early childhood rearing.

Biggles was soon manacled to a bed by the matron, who patted him on the head and threw the key out the window into the pond to prevent him from running away. Then left him to become acquainted with the other ninth form borders.

The other boys in the dorm watched with interest at Biggles who was as foreign as the French kid in grade nine who insisted he was the Dauphin. Biggles held up a cricket bat and demanded a daiquiri and Beef Wellington before he would surrender, none of which made any sense to the other boys who still struggling with the concept of onanism and girlie magazines.

"I'm the famous Biggles!" Biggles attempt a tactic he had found worked when dealing with the Boche and rampaging Jacquerie. This was met with nervous stares. It was his wild eyed stare and the .455 Webley Mark I service revolver strapped to his thigh that had their attention. The matron had removed the ammo so it was useless at shooting the lock off the bed chain or shooting her for that matter. "Anyone? Nothing?"

It was true none of them had the faintest idea who he was, if had used a time machine to the neolithic age he would have been just as unknown. Biggles was a creature from another age, a long forgotten symbol of empire and those jolly good times when white men wore pith helmets and civilization began with high tea in Grosvenor Place then ended in a small cafe outside Verdun.

"Shouldn't you be in tenth form?" one of the more intrepid stupid students attempted to parley. He was so stupid he later graduated as a biologist and was killed when attempting to teach a hippo how to scuba-dive in the London zoo.

"I have money! I have drugs! Just get me out of these!" Biggles rattled the chains on the bed. "I can get you into any brothel in Egypt you want!"

"Do you have the latest Harry Potter book?"

Then the bell rang and it was time for class. This however, broke the back of the hero of the Sopwith Camel. Biggles screamed and bit at his chains: "Cthulhu! Cthulhu is coming!"

Mister McGregor the Geography teacher was, who had one of those wonderfully bland faces that would allow him to to spend the rest of his life being essentially invisible and was so incompetent he was once arrested for being a lamppost. Mister McGregor was a short deliberate fossil left over from an enlightened Dickensian age educational system based on beatings, beatings and occasional mention of how technically America was still part of the Empire. He was also so violent he was known to decapitate students for handing in late essays and had once said "If I could resurrect them as a necromancer I would, then I would kil them all! That's how annoyed I am."

The lessons revolved around the Scotsman McGregor screaming insults about the English to them, beating them with the 1911 edition of the Encyclopedia Brittanica and telling them the true source of the Nile was in Edinburgh.

Biggles dragged his bed into the classroom and propped it against his desk.

"Bigglesworth!" Screamed McGregor. "Where is your essay on the Orinoco Delta?"

Biggles screamed and went into a foetal ball under his bed, and this was the hammer of the Hun, breaker of the Blitzkrieg, buggerer of the Bosch, a man renowned for flying into battle wearing nothing more than a gin and tonic. "Sir I've been absent for over a hundred years, I thought I was past the due date."

"There is no due date in this class. Detention."

Detention started at 11 am while parading on the rugby field, and lasted for the rest of the day. A day in which five of the students went mad in the noonday sun, three convincingly faked malaria and were allowed a visit to the nurse, and two tried to escape but were savaged by the school's hounds before they made the walls. While Biggles was forced to recite Tennyson's Charge of the Light Brigade while gargling marbles and standing on his head.

Hours later the nurse tapped on his bed:

"Bigglesworth come out here now! Its way past tea-time and the cook wants to go home and strangle the wife."

Biggles peaked his head out and realized he had fainted for several hours and was in dire need of liquids, presumably in the form of alcohol wrapped about a dancer from the Folies Bergère.

The geography teacher had disappeared and was replaced by the visage of a woman who had once stampeded Last Night of the Proms into a four day riot that was only ended when Prime Minister Anthony Eden sent in the troops.

"Waaagh!" Biggles hid under the bed again.

"No, come out dearie," the nurse said again with the breath of someone who gargled from the waste water of an Essex brewery. "Classes are over."

"Over? The War is over?" Biggles was immensely relieved, there hadn't been such a sense of relief since the Black Hole of Calcutta had been hushed over as a diplomatic incident.

"What war? Now then none of that nonsense, dinner time."

Dinner comprised a meal prepared by a former sadistic staff sergeant in the French Foreign Legion, comprised entirely of oatmeal baked so hard it reverted to wood, and pudding was oatmeals mixed with diluted offal. Biggles tried feeding it to the school rats but they were having none of it, having learned from long experience it was better to nibble on the boys while they slept. At his point Biggles decided he had had enough and tried hiding under the table but it was no use as the bed still manacled to his leg wouldn't fit.

"Come on dearie, it's time to have your shower and beating. Be a good little soldier and come along."

Part of the rigorous training for the boys, staff and WWI invalids was a ten miles hike with full kit in the dormitory shower while being thrashed with a bundle of birch twigs in a two hundred degree sauna. Boys were known to pass out and die on their first attempt, and once the entire fifth form had gone into cardiac shock when the thermostat had melted from years of overuse. If it wasn't for the excellent therapeutic results of killing off the weaker members of species, it would have been banned years ago. Biggles suffered manly as he could for about ten minutes before he bolted for the door, only to be met the nurse's fist and thrown back in the shower to start over again. From this point on, he ran in circles in the showers, singing "Rule Britannia" and "God Save the Kaiser". It only ended when the birch twigs they thrashed him with melted in the humidity and were deemed too soft on the boy.

Finally he was allowed to drag his bed, still manacled to his leg, into the dorm only to discover the other boys were formulating an escape plan that involved a Wooden Horse and the Siege of Troy. Biggles pointed out the plan only worked if they were on the outside of the castle to start with, they were trying to get in, and more importantly they lacked the logistics to fabricate a Greek army out of bed sheets and pillow cases. He suggested a more reasoned plan, where first they raided the school armoury and equip themselves with the latest breech-loading Martini–Henry rifle of 1872, then kidnap the school's matron at gun point and simply blow a hole in the school's out perimeter. This was met with considerable mutterings of "it wasn't cricket" and "what would Harry Potter do in this situation?". It was only after Biggles had pointed out that two out of every five students died before graduation they agreed to fall in line.

The morning broke and the plan was executed perfectly as Biggles had predicted. The lock to the armoury was smashed, the Martini–Henry rifles were given to all and sundry, and then the school matron was leapt upon by a dozen anaemic boys screaming:

"Zulu! Zulu!"

Then the plan failed miserably as the boys from tenth form were commissioned under the headmaster and beat the lower form into submission with hockey sticks and grenades.

While all this was going on, Biggles reported to the school's Post Office and had the bed, still manacled to his leg, posted to No. 17 Flying Training School at Settling, Norfolk. Which was precisely how he had escaped his old school one hundred years before and joined the Royal Air Force.

James Conor O'Brien is the author of the following books all available on Amazon.com, CreateSpace, and Smashwords

Science Fables Volume I, II, III

A wildly eclectic set of parodies of the great scientists and their life, from Newton the anti-highwayman, Einstein's drug enthused rampage across the Italian Alps, Shakespeare the world's most dyslexic spy, Darwin the Vivisectionist, James Clerk Maxwell reprograms the entire universe, Johannes Kepler and Tycho Brahe encounter a drunken moose and Galileo fools the inquisition. Strangely none of which is recorded in actual biographies but fortunately are here now exposed for the first time in these timeless vignettes.

Excerpt:
--Charles Darwin was seasick, he had been seasick from the first dawn, and he had been so relentlessly seasick for a week now that he was beginning to wonder if his intestines were being attacked by a sea cucumber. This was surprisingly close to the truth, as the ship's cook had been poisoning the entire crew ever since he had come aboard. The cook's approach to cuisine was his revenge on the British navy for having press-ganged him into service from the finest restaurant in Belgravia and carted off to serve slop to drunken sailors aboard the HMS Beagle. Most of the meals consisted of whatever odd animals he could drag from the sea, ranging from albatrosses, vampire squids, and most provocatively ambergris - which for lack of a better title was listed on the menu as vomitus whaleus.

Darwin stared out the porthole. Plymouth sat there as steady as a rock and he wondered if they would ever set to sea. The captain had insisted that before their voyage the officers and gentlemen spent time with each other, it had only taken one meal for them to develop an instinctive dislike of each other and of the dining room. The captain assured them that seasickness was common even among seasoned sailors, and then threw up a curry made up of octopus eyeballs, leafy sea-dragons and malaria tablets.

"Gentlemen, a toast!" captain FitzRoy lifted a glass, "to a successful voyage, and to sweethearts and wives - may they never meet!"

"Could we just have a slice of dry toast?" Darwin groaned.

"What's wrong with the meal?"

"Well, either it's still alive or it has come back from the grave," Darwin pushed the plate away.

"Nonsense," FitzRoy looked annoyed, "the cook is the finest we could press gang from the restaurants of Belgravia. None finer."

"None finer than what?" Darwin watched amazed as the shell of some antediluvian crustacean emerged of its own volition like the Birth of Venus from beneath the soup. --

Skymarine Jones

A frenzied, relentless, comic parody of all space marines and their Torus worlds. A no holds bared, humorous assault on modern science fiction - seriously, that's what it's like. As the hero and his band of drunken, bungling Skymarines blunder from disastrous battle to the next, chased by space pirates, sentient garbage disposals, and cyborg dragons.

Visit the realm that couldn't exist, the Daisy Chain World, the largest artificial megastructure in the galaxy, made from thousands of lesser torus orbitals all spinning at seven kilometres a second in perfect orbit around Saturn. The Daisy Chain so complicated, so non-linear, so peculiar, it needs to be run by a computer so infinite it is housed outside the physical universe. An infinite computer at war with the very world of worlds it is supposed to govern - and is quite, quite, quite mad. Meet Skymarine Jones the accidental general who has part of Einstein's brain stuck in his head, unfortunately it's the part that deals with sex and bowel movements and as often as not leads them in the wrong direction. Listen to the Sentient Gun, a deranged nuclear-powered, robotic, talking Gatling gun - convinced it's possessed by the gods of Haitian Voodou. Walk across civilizations where the idea of rationality has gone the way of the diabetic dinosaur. Join Jonsey and his small army of twelve idiots on the Torus World of all Torus Worlds!

Excerpt:

--The cyborg dragon followed their scent along the road, occasionally stopping to talk to cows and eating them. It would moo at herds of cattle in the fields; it would moo so loud they often as not died of heart attacks. The dragon found this very interesting. It ran into a pod of Tyrannosaurs Rex and tried to play tag with them, but they ran over a cliff in shrieking terror. It had also discovered it could fly, and had a great deal of fun dropping out of the sky like a screaming Stuka, landing next to a brontosaurus and watching it faint.--

Macschrödinger's Cat: The strange tale of the cat and the Universe.

Excerpt: The Philosophy of Quantum Mechanics gate crashes the Mad Hatter's Tea Party. A world where Erwin Schrödinger is a wild red haired Scotsman and the universe we know has nothing to do with reality:

"Gentlemen, my name is MacSchrödinger!" he cried, rolling out the broad Scottish accent, "It was maself who discovered this type of cat yer're been 'erre discussing ... and I think, tha' therre few things yer should need to know abut this 'erre beastie." A deep silence fell into the room as everybody looked expectantly towards the newcomer. He stood spotlighted by the dust sparkling in the beams of light, which shot through the darkness of the room to carve a day in the dark of the theatre. The rabbit woke up and poked its head up over the edge of the box. "As yer very well know indeed," said MacSchrödinger slowly and with distinct care as he made his way down the stairs," a few years ægo while on a big game hunting expedition in Cheshire; on tha dark and terrable continent called England," the 'RRR's' thrilled through the air, "that I first discovered this extraordinary species of Cat!" He spat the word out. "At great risk to myself, mind ye, and with a terrible loss of life to ma hunting party." He now stood in front of them, before the blackboard and resting his hands or the box in which the rabbit cowered within. "Ach, næ doubt yer have read in the popular press," he paused as if to show his contempt of tha' institution," of the extra-orrdinary events that took place on the expedition Of the terrible, terrible battle that took ocurred twixt the camps baker and the deadly, deadly Jabberwocky! And how we lost the self-same baker ir his last heroic final conflict with tha' terrible, terrible Boojum Quark!"

Vladimir

A relentless satire of Russian Presidents since the fall of the Sovie Union. See Vladimir discover air-rifles and the art of accidently killing everything from wolves, tigers, dolphins and prime ministers in a riotou comedy of corruption and mismanagement. Watch Boris waltz into histor in a drunken fugue as he discovers new ways to reinvent détente. Meet the mysterious President Dmitry who is destined to be Russia's only permanent under prime minister. A ravishing satirical exposé of contemporary Russian politics from oligarchs, secretariats, diplomatic incidents and international disasters as Russian President and Prime Ministers stumble helplessly and hopelessly forward to a bright future of Novorossiya.

Excerpt:
--Vladimir had big plans for all of Europe and had filed away those big plans under the title the New Russia. It involved a complex series of political, financial and news media manoeuvres that would completely restructure the whole of Europe to the Russian model. This New Russia was to extend all the way from Odessa on the Black Sea to Finchley Station in North London. Vladimir couldn't explain why he had chosen Finchley Station as the western most border of Novorossiya other than London Bus route 82 terminated there. Scotland, Ireland and Spain would be permanent buffer countries to the Atlantic if the Canadians ever decided to invade. While all of the Nordic states, Germany, France and Italy would join the New Russia as these like the Ukraine were part of the ancient Russian homeland.

No amount of arguments with his psychologist would persuade him otherwise.

"So you are thinking Finchley Station is where Tsar Alexander began his conquest of Turkestan?" Vladimir's psychologist peered over his glasses at his client. "Most interesting, a little odd maybe, but most interesting."

"It was all part of the Great Game between the British and the Russian empires for supremacy in Central Asia Britain," Vladimir lay back upon a Chaise longue and stared at the ceiling. "By placing the western most borders of Russia dead in the heart of London, Tsar Alexander was able to outwit Queen Victoria and steal a march on Colonial Indian Army."

The psychologist blew a smoke ring and made a note. "You know, President Vladimir," he tried diplomatically, "it does seem a little implausible. I mean just because the Tsar said Finchley Station was part of the Russia doesn't really mean it was part of the Russian empire. It could have been a metaphor or even a joke at Queen Victoria's expense."

Vladimir looked annoyingly at his physician. Vladimir had gimlets for eyes when he was annoyed, no one actually knows what gimlets for eyes means, but if anyone is going to have gimlets for eyes it is going to be Vladimir.

"You must remember," the would-be-world-leader growled, "anywhere the Russian peoples have lived, then that land becomes part of the great Russian Motherland."

"Including Finchley Station?"

"Especially Finchley Station!"--

Peter Pan Bedtime Stories: The Boy Who Forgot How To Fly

A playful tender retelling of J.M.Barrie's eternal story of Never Land where Peter, Wendy, Pixies and the Lost Boys continue their joyful adventures with pirates, moonbeams and dreams. This book is the perfect bedtime story for sending the littleun's off to sleep, filled with adventures, magic, wonderful and joy. Just what ever child should be read to as they fall asleep.

Excerpt:

Snow came to the woods, it lay deep, deep enough to drown the grass and give chilblains to elephants. Pixies hated snow, not because they suffer from chilblains, or dislike white things, mainly because they hated the way snowflakes kept knocking their hats off. They sat on the branch of an oak tree, on the edge of the Great Forest; as it stretched farther than anyone could imagine, no matter how many days you traipsed through it, you could never reach the other side. Which was a bit odd, as you could sail around the Island of Never-Never in a single day, provided the wind was being polite that day, and you didn't run into any pirates. In the mist of winter you could hear moose and boar bashing their way through the forest, wolves howled on the tops of mountains like wild winds, and Maggs and Tink struggled to keep up with the day's quota.

No two snowflakes are the same, and neither are two pixies:

"It's upside down," Maggs pointed out.

"How can you tell?" Tink quizzed.

"The squiggly bit at the top."

"But that's the bottom."

"How can you tell?"

"Because I'm holding it back to front."

"Ah," finished Maggs, the wiser of the two.

The art of making snowflakes is so obscure, so baffling, and so mysterious – that I won't even bother to explain. Suffice to say it requires cold, rain and a lot of annoyed pixies shivering in the winter. Snowflakes are made by pixies, it's their trade, and like all jobs they hated it.

"Shall I give it a bob?" asked Tink.

"Oh no, frosttwizzles don't have them." said Maggs. Frosttwizzles was the name they gave to snowflakes. "They have bells."

"They do?"

"Why yes," insisted Maggs as she held up a small bell.

"Hey, that's from my hat!"

There is a reason why no two snowflakes are exactly the same; it is because pixies can never agree or even remember how to make them. As they sat, snowflakes kept falling out of the sky and thumping them on their heads. Scott of the Antarctic never had to suffer such a pickle.

"Oh!" popped Tink as her head shook from another knock on her noggin. "Drat these frosttwizzles!"

You may be wondering why pixies make snowflakes when they hate them so much, well I don't know. No one knows the mind of a pixie, least of all the pixies themselves.

Before them in the snow stood an ice palace they built, earlier in the day, it glittered in the sunlight like a chandelier.

"Do you think we need huskies?" asked Maggs gluing another icicle to her mess.

"What are they?"

"For the dogsled."

"We have a dogsled?"

"Yes, we are exploring today."

"Won't they eat us?"

"Never! We will have nice huskies, the kind you can take to picnics and discover the South Pole."

"Gosh in that case, let's get huskies," agreed Tink brightly. "You know, modern art is all bosh."

"Yes I think so," said Maggs and held up a snowflake in the shape of a duck.

"Brilliant!" said Tink.

They set off to discover the South Pole. Their dogsled turned out to be a large tulip tied to two ladybirds, who were jolly annoyed at being woken up in the middle of their Winter hibernation to take a couple of tipsy pixies on a traipse around the lake.

"What shall we call our huskies?" asked Tink.

"Icecow and Snowbean," grinned Maggs.

The two ladybirds looked grimly at each other, but said nothing; they had no choice as they pixies had put horse bits in their mouths. The expedition was the result of minutes of planning and seconds of discussion; everything was left to chance.

James Conor O'Brien also studied physics at the University of Queensland and is the author of Dynamical Casimir Effect and the Big Bang, a paper on the evolution of matter from the Big Bang. c.f. following blog

http://revolutionmatter.blogspot.com.au/2014/07/an-introduction-to-revolution-of-matter.html

This is the blurb where I try and sell other books because I like to eat and pay rent, you have no idea how annoying it is for me to do other things than writing books. So if you find this book humorous, and technically that would make me a comedian, and you have been able to ignore all the grammar and spelling errors, then please buy one of my books.

For the love of comedy buy one - I'm wasting away here!

My blog is at : http://reeddebuch.blogspot.com.au/

I live on a wombat farm in the outer suburbs of Melbourne, since in recent years the price of wombats have fallen I have taken to using them as get away vehicles in smash and grab raids on curbside lemonade stalls.

CPSIA information can be obtained
at www.ICGtesting.com
Printed in the USA
BVHW04s0904130918
527278BV00042B/378/P

9 781519 529022